I0600773

BEN BROEREN

Sour Pineapples in Paradise

First published by Benjamin D. Broeren 2018

Copyright © 2018 by Ben Broeren

All rights reserved. No part of this publication may be reproduced, stored or transmitted in any form or by any means, electronic, mechanical, photocopying, recording, scanning, or otherwise without written permission from the publisher. It is illegal to copy this book, post it to a website, or distribute it by any other means without permission.

This novel is entirely a work of fiction. The names, characters and incidents portrayed in it are the work of the author's imagination. Any resemblance to actual persons, living or dead, events or localities is entirely coincidental.

Cover images courtesy of Pixabay, edited using open source GNU Image Manipulation Program.

First edition

ISBN: 978-0-9977761-1-9

This book was professionally typeset on Reedsy. Find out more at reedsy.com

To those who enjoy good stories, perseverance, and a thirst for knowledge.

Acknowledgement

This story is possible thanks to many friends and family.

My good friend, Mark Marohl, helped copy edit and add insights to my narrative from its first draft until publishing. Thanks, Mark. Until the next time.

A number of cousins added their perspective to help the novel along. Thank you. I take responsibility if I've misrepresented your sensibilities.

Cody Broeren, a Marine veteran, helped me with some authenticity into the mind of soldiers and veterans. He also gave a glance at some of the action scenes. Semper Fi, Cody.

José R. Sanchez assisted with my many questions about Puerto Rican Spanish, affirming and correcting my discoveries of our fellow US citizens on the island. Continuaré llamándote "Big Cojones." jajaja…

Tim Broeren helped with his knowledge of firearms and interest in thrillers. Keep on teaching the next generation how to get things done, cousin.

Many thanks also go out to all library staff and booksellers who work to spread knowledge, culture, and a safe space to explore. In particular, thanks to the Chicago Public Library, my wife Caroline, and former coworkers Jamaal, Edwin, Ms. Janet, Ms. Belinda, Svetlana, Derek, Ryan, K, and others.

In the course of research for this story, I found the following book of particular value: *Harvest of Empire : a History of Latinos in America,* by Juan Gonzalez. If you wish to learn more about Latin America, the U.S., and Puerto Rico in particular, please check it out at your local bookstore or library.

Last but not least, thanks to my readers and all others who appreciate a good story.

1

Rumble in the Jungle

Ron Riley had been in a similar situation before. Thugs with performance-enhanced egos had again taken him captive. As he woke up with a sack over his head, blurred visions flashed underneath still opening eyelids. The trail of saliva or blood dripping from his lips also tasted of *déjà vu*. He was coming off of some sort of sedative, and not the fun-filled kind. The spinning sensation in his head wasn't imagined.

Three circumstances made this experience different from the past. His legal surname had been McCallister before WITSEC "protection." His abductors spoke Spanish instead of English. Also, due to the feel of the terrain, he figured he was likely in the back seat of a sedan-like car traveling at more than sixty miles per hour on a highway in Puerto Rico.

It was less likely that government spooks were behind his abduction. Weren't they supposed to be agents of protection? He couldn't rule anything out.

"I'm gonna have to defy some assholes," Ron mumbled to himself in barely a whisper. He realized his hands were zip-tied in front of him. "I gotta take care of this first."

The cozy space around him shook and Ron figured the car had taken a sharp turn. He reached his right hand to the upper band of his left sock. Even if he ordinarily carried a gun on him, the most incompetent of thugs would've taken it. He suspected they wouldn't have found the small Schrade pocket knife hidden next to his ankle. Their oversight made him grin.

The relaxed, but pleasantly passionate, Cuban-infused melody of "Dos Gardenias" filtered through the radio up front as Ron began his struggle with the small knife to cut through the thick plastic. Tito Puente's "Oye Como Va," which followed, was more appropriate as strokes of the blade followed the beat of muted trumpets. It was enough to free his hands. Despite a few nicks to his thumb, he gave another grin under the sack before returning the knife to its hiding space.

"Time to form a plan," Ron mouthed the words to himself before a tire blew and the vehicle came to a sudden stop. "Shit."

Ron couldn't decide if he was thankful or not when a stream of automatic gunfire hit the hood. He had another enemy...or a helper. Either way, there was a distraction thrown into the mix if he wanted to make a run for it.

Ron swung his fists toward the back door when it opened. Whoever he hit returned the favor before the sack was re-moved. The punch and harsh light smacked him before he was dragged to the ground outside. He bit the inside of his cheek in hopes any adrenaline and cortisol would wake him up from the hit, any disorientation, and the residual effects of sedatives.

Two tan-skinned figures came into view, crouching next to him. A mustachioed face spit out accented, rapid-fire English he had to struggle to understand.

"Señor Riley, I wanna guarantee you safety if you cooperate," mustache said. "We need to ask some questions. You gotta stay calm as–"

Ron ducked when automatic weapons fire knocked mustache down, leaving the man with nasty shots to the stomach. The other *Boricua* grabbed his own weapon, which happened to be a Springfield 1911, an FBI SWAT team sidearm. The man grabbed Ron's arm, pushing him toward the Dodge sedan in which they'd arrived.

Within a second, the Springfield-wielding tough guy rolled the wounded to cover. All three edged as quickly and as closely as they could behind the driver's side trunk. At least the engine didn't appear on fire.

Trees and dense foliage surrounded them along a highway Ron recognized as one of those en route to San Juan. If he wasn't the focus of gunfire, the jungle would have presented an advantage. Instead, he froze as rounds from the automatic ripped through the back window just above his head.

"Coño," his company muttered under his breath. The man with FBI firepower did a quick sign of the cross over the wounded, who appeared unconscious or dead.

Ron took out his pocket knife before shushing, with all due diplomacy, the operative who'd abducted him. He was fairly certain bravado wasn't his best move, at least not yet. Manners were difficult enough off the battlefield.

"Trust me; *confía en mí*," he said. *"Soy un gringo de los buenos."*

The man opposite gave him a toothy smile before shaking his Springfield for emphasis. He then gestured a straightened middle finger on the other hand.

Ron didn't have to work hard to suppress any amusement. In ordinary times, he'd chuckle at the man's *cojones*. Being kidnapped and shot at killed any levity. He folded back the blade and lifted it just above the car, rotating it to reflect the sunlight.

The move was met with another stream of automatic fire that resulted in one of the Dodge's side mirrors being shot to pieces. The Schrade's blade was withdrawn just in time.

"Asshole," Ron muttered before his current company gave a thumbs up. He then had to stifle a chuckle when his new acquaintance brought out an M84 flash-bang grenade from his field vest.

Ron attempted to locate their machismo enemy with what was left of the mirror on his side. He tried not to reflect sunlight as his *compadre* held the pin of the M84.

Just after automatic weapons fire again rattled above their heads, the flash-bang was thrown in the direction of cadenced shots. Ron liked to think the non-lethal grenade helped but didn't waste time confirming. He was too busy running toward the promise of dense foliage he could see on the other side of the highway.

For what it mattered, he hoped that the flash-bang throwing fella could also take the chance to escape. The preparedness and courage under fire were worthy of respect.

* * *

The soldier, *la soldado*, squatted between two ferns, over one hundred yards from the Dodge. The flash-bang had thrown her off, but she regained control of the situation in the seconds the *gringo* had taken run away from the FBI man. The Fed just stayed hidden by the slowly deteriorating Dodge.

She could have sniped Ron and then the Fed protecting him if she'd been given the proper tools. If she had complete control of the situation, she would've chosen an M24 sniper rifle rather than the MAC-10 provided. Her boss knew surprisingly little about guns for being a *narco.*

La soldado still deferred to those who paid her. She still had the option of making sure there was one less FBI agent in the world. She relished the challenge without any thought to moral questions, happy to still have a spare magazine, but regretting having left the other at a drop site.

The FBI agent shot his .45. He missed by a good twenty yards, but his tenacity and semblance of skill impressed her. She then released another stream of bullets toward the Dodge. She watched through sights as the agent tossed another flash-bang. She braced herself this time and shut her light brown eyes before impact.

Adrenaline pumped through *la soldado*'s petite, but chiseled frame as she fired again. An iciness ran through the back of her neck when a few rounds returned from the .45 ripped only several feet above her head.

After switching to the last magazine, she shot a slew of bullets toward where the agent had been hiding. His return volley grazed her shoulder in a show of skill, luck, or more likely combination of both.

She shot in the direction of the .45 until she was almost out of ammo before deciding to flee. She hadn't killed the primary target, Ron Riley, so she wasn't expecting any pay. The Fed impressed her, but pangs of adversity and adventure rushed through her veins as she jogged away to kill another day.

When she was a mile or so east, she disassembled the MAC-10 at a drop point, tore off a sleeve of her camouflage jacket and used part of the cloth to wrap the pieces of the automatic before burial with the other magazine. She took another torn piece of her jacket and wrapped her wound, tugging her sweaty tank top around the getup before continuing with a jog. She could regroup at a safe house in the southern San Juan neighborhood of Río Piedras.

In time, she stopped at a tenement off of Calle Azucena and gave two quick knocks. Two dark eyes peered through a sliding panel.

"*Ayuda, maricón,*" *la soldado* said to the man inside. Help, you pansy.

In the nondescript building, she made her way to a unit on the second floor for which she had a key. Once there, she grabbed a fifth of cheap *ron blanco* from a high cupboard.

She poured some of the rum down her caramel-skinned throat as her chest took in more relaxed breaths. The sting of the alcohol poured on her shoulder made her wince, but was needed to disinfect. She took a Motorola Razr from a dresser drawer and entered the constantly changing number of a burner phone.

"*Sí, patrón,*" she said as her boss greeted her. She listened for further instruction rather than waste time describing the sting of her flesh wound or bruised ego.

The boss bored her enough to bring calm again. She was still irritated with her failure to kill Ron and the agent, soothed only with booze and blame on insufficient tools to get the job done. The Fed saved himself by tapping into her instinct for self-preservation.

A smirk stopped her from laughing when she thought about how easily she could kill her boss. She could wring his scrawny, but cocky neck without breaking a sweat. She still listened attentively. He paid her, after all.

"*Eres linda, incluso si a veces decepcionas,*" he said to her before they disconnected. Even disappointments can be beautiful.

La soldado tore off what remained of the bloodied black tank top. She started a brisk shower before removing her camouflage cargo pants and whatever was underneath. She'd have to rely on cold water and rum to hold her over until her boss arranged delivery of cash and cannabis later in the evening.

The rum helped as she applied sterile gauze and a freshly washed handkerchief over the wound. She would be safe for now.

She slipped into a pair of boyshorts and rested her body on a cleanish cot. The adrenaline had left. The warmth of the booze and the air around her beckoned for a nap.

2

Good Housekeeping

Supervisory Special Agent Matt Russo scratched his wrists and sweated in the FBI Miami field office. In front of his Toshiba laptop, he read the latest marching orders in search of evidence. He missed a more active role, working off actionable intelligence on the ground to take down thugs. Sitting on his ass, delegating tips to agents with similar chiseled frames and crew cuts, though lacking the same gumption, was his current lot.

In a memo on the laptop's screen, he read how the head of one of the evidence response teams justified saber-rattling toward Latino Miami *narcos.* The influence of desk jockeys in the DEA rustled through the plodding prose promoting a policy of preemption.

Russo had to stifle a yawn before typing his own memo for his team to remain vigilant. A beer and a cigarette would've helped his mood temporarily, but his wife Clara was a strict stickler against such slip-ups in his newfound sobriety.

It had been one hundred twenty-two days since his last sip of booze.

He knew she was right, so he instead picked at a bag of sunflower seeds he kept in his left-hand drawer. The notice from his secretary about an incoming collect call from San Juan on line two gave him a momentary glimpse of excitement. It was what he needed more than a shot of bourbon.

"Agent Russo," he said.

"Hey, ya pencil pusher," Ron responded over the phone. "How's tricks in Miami? I don't trust the locals with this, so I thought I'd call an old buddy stateside. I'll give you a call later? We should talk. How's the old battle ax and kid?"

Russo said a four-letter word before grudgingly giving his home mobile and hanging up.

Getting involved with Ron Riley, aka McCallister, was the last thing Clara wanted for their new perfect life in the Coconut Grove neighborhood of Miami. The Russos had had to flee their previous life after Matt Russo and Ron had worked together to bring down the Chicago mob. Miami was nicer for the family for more than just the better climate temperatures.

With Agent Russo's non-life-threatening position as an armchair patriot assisting the diminished, more politically correct leftovers of the War on Drugs, his daughter, Zoe, could attend a good charter school and the three of them didn't have to worry about getting shot at. Well, at least gunfire wasn't an issue in their neighborhood.

Apart from Clara's Yoga instruction and "enrichment activities" for Zoe, she worked as a personal banker at a Florida Community Bank branch. Federal help from the Great Recession was about to put his wife in high demand for those still interested in putting their money under an institutional mattress. Fear of markets before Spring 2009 added some excitement to her work, at least.

Russo would welcome their domestic bliss more if he could do some field or investigative work where he didn't feel as if his balls were being cut off. He was a veteran still trying to serve his country, but he felt more like an underutilized, underpaid machinist still grinding away in the Rust Belt.

He loved his ladies, but the tranquility of calm, family, and obligations made him want to reenlist in the Army at times. For some reason, working with a platoon in a Middle Eastern country made an iota more of sense.

Dinner at home and the bedtime routine for Zoe called him to a more nuanced, perhaps more healthy place. His beautiful wife and daughter needed him to be in the present. He had passion and duty as a father and husband.

Still, Agent Matt Russo anticipated Ron's call like a service dog does for commands and raw, red meat.

* * *

Carey Riley chopped potatoes and plantains in her and her husband, Ron's, kitchen in Fajardo, Puerto Rico, along the east coast of the US commonwealth island. She had just changed into flip-flops, navy blue shorts, and a white button-down, putting her crimson, shoulder length hair into a relaxed ponytail. Her son, John, was watching a Spanish-dubbed version of Dora the Explorer in the next room. She sipped a freshly made mojito and ran a hand along tense muscles in her fair-skinned neck.

The latent strain was a reminder that two hours earlier, she'd answered her mobile phone to a breathless Ron, who only said he was outside a Pueblo Supermarket just west of Carolina, toward San Juan. The call came from a public payphone.

Her boss at the gun range had been displeased to let her leave work early, but she was persuasive. She let the guy get a glimpse of her healthy cleavage and said that she had to get home for her man; target practice could wait. *Una mujercita* could work her assets.

Ron had refused to meet her for fear of fallout from his run-in with highway bandits along the rainforest. He really didn't care for Carey's boss, at any rate.

"Well, hon," Ron had said over the phone, "I'm in the thick of it again. You'll excuse me if I don't make it home for dinner. I want to keep gun-toting assholes away from you, John, and the house."

"You're lucky you make a good drink and are good in the sack," Carey said. "If you don't return in one piece to your family, I'll find you in the afterlife."

"Yes, dear," he said. "I'd rather be there keeping house, prepping dinner and drinks. But I've got thugs on the hunt."

"Sounds familiar. Love ya."

"Igualmente, mi amor."

After the phone call and before returning to their beach home in Fajardo, she had walked to John's preschool to escort her son home and to keep worries out of her mind.

Carey and Ron had been friends and lovers, exchanging favors both amorous and otherwise, last year while evading mobsters in the Chicago suburbs. She eventually took his name, McCallister, before being renamed Riley courtesy of WITSEC. Then came relocation to Puerto Rico. Risk and thrills were no strangers to them.

"Only those who dare to fail greatly can ever achieve greatly," she mumbled to herself in the moment.

She wasn't about to let him die now but figured Ron would

do what he could to protect family. Ron was a decent father figure to her son, competent in the kitchen, and knew how to make her tic in the bedroom.

She finished sauteing dinner in the pan and called John to eat with her. Worries ran through her mind, and she left them to soak along with the pans. Focusing on what she could control made her feel better.

Carey forced a smile around her son and enjoyed the routine to pretend that everything was normal. John helped her play the part when he switched off the TV and set the dinner table without having to be told. She kissed him on the forehead before they ate and chatted in Spanish and English about their days.

The atmosphere was peaceful until moments after John's bedtime.

3

Are you Giving me the Business?

Ron was hopeful. Exhausted, but hopeful

Despite being tied up in the back seat of a Dodge by someone who looked like a jaded FBI agent and being shot at with an automatic, the events were a welcome change of scenery.

It wasn't that tending bar in Fajardo and catching occasional criminal intel to help innocents was boring, but a part of him missed racing to stay alive.

The rattling of the automatic had jarred his nerves and jogged his memory. The person shooting was likely better trained than any Iraqi insurgents who'd shot at him five years earlier in Mosul. The lack of rules for engagement this time around was liberating and scary at the same time. His survival took precedence over killing anyone, but that didn't instill peace of mind.

He regretted being absent for the best part of his day, playing house with his wife and their son before dinner and drinks. Ron pictured Carey and John cleaning up after dinner, her reclining near her son in bed and reading *The Cat in the Hat* before shutting out the lights. He longed to join her for a shower and a snuggle.

Evolving to present dangers kept him from home. Ron purchased a Nokia burner at a store near the Pueblo, texted the new number to Carey, and made a phone call he hoped would help. He and his old FBI buddy, Agent Matt Russo, had kept up through anonymous accounts and personal email.

"Hey, pisshead, how's tricks at your undisclosed location?" Russo asked upon answering. "Also, calling collect from San Juan? It's a good thing there are no ties between the mob and federal government. "

If the sarcasm was meant to sting, it didn't succeed. They were well past an argument over respecting rules and regulations.

"Local, official-looking thugs shoved me in the trunk of a car and someone tried to give me a haircut with automatic gunfire to disrupt my relaxed life in the tropics," Ron said. "So I'm throwing protocol to the wind. By the way, have you enjoyed any charity golf outings lately?"

Russo said a four-letter word before asking Ron for details. The clank of ice cubes in a glass echoed in the background.

Ron gave his point of view of the late morning and early afternoon activities. The story included the use of his Schrade knife, scuffling with captors telling him to be calm, assistance by a Spanish-speaker whom he suspected was FBI due to the Springfield sidearm, and his escape from a well-trained, automatic-armed psycho. His one-man audience rattled ice cubes on his end, poured something from a bottle, and gave a sigh. Then came another four-letter word for good measure.

"So, how are the wife and daughter?" Ron asked again. "They must not be near with your potty mouth and hitting the sauce."

"God damn it, Ron," Russo responded. "Zoe and Clara

went to bed early and I'm listening to a lunatic rave about jungle kidnappings and potential government conspiracies. My libations aren't the issue here."

"Hey, call it concern for an old pal. My wifey's probably done putting the kid to bed. It's no fun drinking alone. Could you help a brother out and look at my issues from your side as a Fed? I'm awfully fond of my family and need to wrap up any loose ends before getting back in touch."

"I'll have a look at personnel, news, and intranet chatter...on my own time. Keep C and J safe, scour the papers, and wait for my call. And don't friggin' call me collect again from your WITSEC location."

"Yes, sir. Want me send you Cohibas if Castro falls in Cuba?"

Again with the four-letter words.

Ron and Russo chatted for a while from different parts of the hemisphere. The back and forth reached a normal, cordial clip before they got to jokes about wops and micks. They ended the conversation with a promise to do brunch soon.

After Ron disconnected, a text returned from Carey put him on edge. It only said, *"Ayuda!"* with a photo attachment of her distressed face. Within a minute, he found a cab to take him to Fajardo. After getting dropped off a few blocks from the house he shared with Carey and John, he snuck to their back door and went inside. He found someone else had taken Carey's place in the living room.

* * *

The body in the armchair near the couch was familiar, but not an acquaintance. Ron had last seen the same midriff-bearing, caramel-skinned, peasant top-wearing gal outside the watering hole where he worked in Fajardo. El Rococo wasn't much classier than his last official job, a bouncer at a suburban Chicagoland strip club. However, the Latin music was better than recycled boy band crap and at least as good as Van Halen.

Ron hadn't expected the prostrate bodies of young women to follow him south of the US mainland. At once, he rushed to the side of the house where he hoped to see his son. A sound-sleeping John made him gasp in relief. His first steps afterward were to see if anyone else was in the house

With John still asleep in his left arm and a loaded Beretta M9 retrieved from a high cupboard in his right hand, Ron crept around the house. He checked closets and shadows before engaging the deadbolt out front and checking all the windows, having to close and lock one in the bathroom.

After laying John underneath his own bed with the gentleness of a well-trained bull terrier, he returned to the living room to figure out more about his unexpected visitor. He diverted his focus to detract from worries about Carey.

Beneath ebony locks running along a still graceful, smooth-skinned neck, Ron checked the carotid artery of the gal reclining in his living room. His ears were listening for any other unexpected visitors as he read a faint, still-present pulse.

He recognized her as a low-rent call girl who made extra money servicing or snitching for local *policía*. One of those was a pal of his in the state police named Carlos Velez. The working lady was an informant for him about local gossip on drugs and organized crime.

Ron then checked a pocket rising and falling slowly under the girl's loosely fitting bust line. Inside was a slip of paper and five single US dollar bills. He placed the sweat-moistened bills on the floor and noticed a small number of track marks in the space between her bicep and forearm. The slip of paper had a note. It read:

We have your wife. If you don't want her to get the same as this puta, *don't call the* policía, *lie low, do what we say. We'll send a messenger tomorrow morning. A negro will collect the* puta's *body. Stay quiet with your son. We're always watching.*

Ron crumpled the note in his fist before letting it fall. His first instinct was to check to see if he could spot the surveillance, then he thought of John and Carey and resigned himself to cooperate. He slid his Beretta under the couch for now and moved to check on his visitor.

The call girl's sweat was cool despite the heat to the air. Her breaths were further apart, her fingertips were turning a shade of blue, and a check of her pupils under still eyelids showed pinprick points. He had to move quickly.

Ron got a jug of water from the fridge and relocated his son to the couch. The boy was too tired to argue, which was a plus.

He wanted to keep the call girl alive. He figured the gal might be able to answer some questions. A four-letter-word from his lips preceded the fact that he hadn't an emergency dose of Narcan.

Ron lifted the girl to the floor while reviewing first aid in his head. When the girl's breaths became too shallow and the pulse fainter, he'd start chest compressions and breaths. With his son and his Beretta right next to him, he expected a long night.

In the early morning, the girl gasped a name, "Fernando."

Ron collapsed on the floor in front of the couch, unable to continue with his energy depleted. He engaged the safety on the Beretta before John climbed down to be with him.

She died just before sunrise.

4

Recon

Agent Roberto Lopez stirred at the crack of dawn in a crumbling brick apartment building off of Calle Azucena in the Río Piedras neighborhood of San Juan. The mud-stained, black and white checkered floor was his only mattress, with the sweat and blood-stained kevlar vest serving as a pillow. He realized he was alone, if not necessarily safe.

He rinsed his face under tepid water flowing from a mold-stained faucet in the rat's nest where he was squatting. Yesterday's events ran through his mind as he realized he needed caffeine and a plan. His supervisor at the FBI and his gut told him to lie low, follow the blood, and figure out why he'd found himself in the middle of a shoot out.

Assistant Special Agent-in-Charge Rodriguo de Salinas was the man to whom he officially answered. Yesterday's orders were to take a *gringo* to an off-the-books interrogation site west of San Juan for questioning about local drug traffickers. He had been ordered to take the asset against his will and keep him in the dark. Lopez and a comrade had done so.

After a low-dose sedative administered to the *gringo* while he had been walking outside his Fajardo house, Lopez and the fellow agent put him in the backseat of a Dodge company car. Everything was gravy before the hijacking.

A MAC-10 toting *loco* had fired rounds toward them to knock down Lopez's coworker. Then, the crafty *gringo* used his knife and Lopez used his FBI-issued sidearm and flash-bang grenades to fight back. He lost his captive amid the chaos.

After a second flash-bang and another eruption of automatic rounds, Lopez had continued to gauge his Springfield toward the noise. His successful shot surprised him more than the fact he was still alive. He aimed afterward and listened. Within minutes, he heard another body running through the foliage. He rushed with what he had on him to stalk his erstwhile predator.

After a mile or so of running, Lopez's quarry disassembled a MAC-10, ditched it in a freshly dug pit, and tore a camouflage sleeve to stem the blood flow. He was surprised to find that the shooter was *una mujer*. He had to smirk after he realized he was averting his eyes while she adjusted her tank top. He followed her until she stopped at a place up the street in an abandoned building.

From his current digs just down the street, he had called Agent de Salinas to confirm the current course of action, or inaction, depending on one's patience. He had also requested help for his severely wounded comrade. State Police and emergency technicians had already responded, or so he'd been told. Exhaustion had followed until the present.

As the morning sun showed, he realized he had to take care of base needs if he wanted to stay effective. Lopez tested the water for potability before he spat it out and decided to take advantage of a nearby convenience store. He descended a flight of wooden stairs patched with dry rot, exited the building's front door, and walked a half block west, closer to where the *mujer* gunslinger was staying.

Inside the store, he bought a liter of Coca-Cola, a copy of the *San Juan Star,* and a granola bar, paying the ancient cashier while keeping his eyes on the street. He hadn't eaten in over twelve hours, so he welcomed the impending rush of caffeine, oats, peanut, and high-fructose corn syrup more than he should have. The air outside was already muggy.

The shooter's building didn't look much nicer than where Lopez squatted. The only visitor since he'd been on stakeout was an ebony-skinned man with a skin-tight, black T-shirt and straw pork pie hat who had delivered a brown paper bag the evening before. Pork pie's pecks and cantaloupe-sized biceps made him appear much too formidable to be an errand boy, and the muscle hadn't lingered or asked for a tip.

Lopez finished his Coke as he looked to a second story window where the soldier, *la soldado,* was staying. He flinched, trying to give casual attention to the *Star* when he saw a figure emerge from a small balcony to look down at the world. His peripheral view trained itself on any movement.

Out of the corner of his eye, he saw a bare set of sporty, smallish breasts through French windows that made him pay closer attention. He gave a quick glance to see a short, sinewy, well-toned frame. From the shooter's left hand the smoldering tip of a joint cut through the haze floating out the window and mirrored the still submissive sunlight from the East.

The air took on the smell of burning wet hay, prompting Lopez to make his way back to his rat's nest to maintain surveillance with an iota of greater interest. He'd smoked cannabis before Quantico, but needed to distance himself to stay sharp. The spartan feel of a dingy apartment provided a good environment to focus on duty.

After climbing creaky stairs to his perch, the undercover FBI agent watched the figure of his quarry, having to stifle a slight degree of excitement below his waist.

In the environs of dirt, filth, and evicted livelihoods, Lopez reminded himself that the *mujer* had almost made him a human colander yesterday. The memory helped him keep a more hostile eye on her after relieving his bladder in a filthy sink that ran to the ground below.

* * *

Matt Russo awoke in his two-bedroom condo in the Coconut Grove neighborhood of Miami next to a T-shirt clad Clara, well aware she had nothing underneath. The two had made love the previous evening before he had taken the phone call from his degenerate pal in Puerto Rico.

Ron's call had given him with a needed rush of adrenaline after the lady beside him reminded Russo of the comforts of home. His principles weren't enough to keep him from his hidden stash of Old Crow bourbon after his wife and daughter were in dreamland. A strong tooth brushing and five hours of unconsciousness allowed him a veneer of control.

Matt Russo was in alpha male mode, and his wife didn't complain during a quick snuggle session. The story he sold himself wasn't entirely fiction. He left her to snooze as he got busy as the sun began its march to show rays in the morning sky.

He first snagged a cup of brew from the programmed

Mr. Coffee before firing up the Toshiba laptop in his home office. FBI intranet showed surveillance on Puerto Rican Independence groups. Digital gossip about their ties to Venezuela's Hugo Chavez and Iran's Mahmoud Ahmadinejad made Russo snicker as he held off the impulse to sneeze Kirkland-brand, Columbian fair-trade coffee out through his nose.

Other traffic about the San Juan municipal police cooperation with Assistant Special Agent-in-Charge Rodriguo de Salinas to address unrest on the ground registered more. Agent de Salinas was highlighted several times as spearheading efforts to work with patriotic locals to root out corruption, or fight local dissent, depending on one's perspective.

The *Boricua* FBI darling worked with a police force known for its shady deals and abuse of the public trust. Images of Russo's previous boss, now convicted felon, former Special Agent-in-Charge Dave Holbert, flew through his head as he considered the potential for a conspiracy between de Salinas, corrupt cops, and other bad actors. Past was prologue.

A search of local blogs showed pictures of a bloody, and bullet-ridden Dodge on a route to San Juan. Not a word of the ambush was mentioned on more official news websites, CNN, FOX NEWS, or even NPR.

Matt Russo felt compelled to dig further. Eventually, he'd have to speak further with Ron about events on the ground. For now, he compelled himself to enjoy family life before the bureaucratic boredom that would greet him at the office. He missed being back in the field, but love for his wife and daughter prevailed.

Sounds of domesticity tugged at his ears, beckoning a calmer reality.

Clara was in Zoe's bedroom, waking her up with a rendition of "Here Comes the Sun" as Matt Russo maneuvered and clicked his touchpad to close browser windows on growing local collusion and resistance to the War on Drugs.

After filling mugs for himself and Clara with the output from Mr. Coffee, he got Pop Tarts for Zoe, Grape Nuts for his wife, and Quaker instant oatmeal for himself. Santana's "Black Magic Woman" over the CD player gave the mood for a droll breakfast.

Matt Russo loaded the dishwasher before he and his women took turns in the bathrooms. With teeth brushed, fresh clothes, a hybrid car, and a Ford sedan, the Russos were the picture of yuppie good citizens.

Zoe and Clara both kissed Supervisory Special Agent Matt Russo at the door before they all started their days.

5

Dirty Deeds, Done Dirt Cheap

Ron awoke in Fajardo to the sound of John crying. A flurry of dread met a dull discomfort as he regained his senses and took stock of his surroundings. A dead call-girl was in his living room, his wife had been abducted, and John was in his stepfather's custody, if just as unhappy with the situation.

After hugging the boy and leading him to the john to relieve himself, Ron poured a cup of fatty, boxed milk for the little man. Ron retrieved his Beretta from underneath the couch, checked the safety, and started French press coffee for himself.

There wasn't much to do but kill time. After John had finished some milk and Ron had some morning brew, he shaved, did push-ups with his son, and the two washed. Ron's Beretta was always within reach. The two men donned clean undershirts, matching tropical button-downs, and khaki-colored cargo shorts. Ron then covered the dead call girl with a sheet and tried to talk things through with John.

"Where's Mom?" he asked. "Who's the sleeping lady? Do I get a day off of school?"

Ron told him Carey had to visit a friend, he didn't know who the lady was, and that school was closed for the day. When John asked why to each of those answers, Ron asked questions in return to keep the boy busy. They both needed a plan.

Ron remembered that their neighbor, an older, stocky native with only a few words of English had been chummy with Carey and the boy. He tried to remember her name, contemplating whether he could trust her with the boy's safety. Three loud knocks on the door startled his train of thought.

With the Beretta in his right hand, Ron motioned for John to hide before he moved to the door to crack it open an inch. The man outside stood on the front stoop ahead of a large roller board suitcase that could fit at least one dead call girl. The visitor struck him as too friendly for comfort. It wasn't what he expected, but he figured that was the point.

The ebony-skinned stranger had a shaved head and wore a lopsided grin that clashed with a black T-shirt and camouflage cargos clinging to his muscled frame. A pork pie hat, liable to be concealing some sort of small pistol, was perched in hands meeting in front of his waist.

"*Puedo ayudarte?*" Ron asked, showing his face. May I help you?

"Yes you can, *señor*," the man said softly, his brown eyebrows showing a friendly crease. "You have *la chica*? *El patrón* wants the exchange clean and simple. If you keep the boy and yourself peaceful, the girl will disappear and I'll give you a note with a time and a place. You show up at six p.m., and we'll go from there. *Entiendes*? Understand?"

Ron wanted to shove the pork pie hat and whatever it was concealing up the stranger's colon, but the subtle professionalism exuded by the smug smile gave him pause. That, and he didn't know where Carey was and didn't figure he'd find out if he pushed his luck. He responded with fake charm to hide his unease, putting his Beretta in his back waistband and giving a stupid smile of his own.

"*Hermano*, please come in," Ron said while raising his volume and the palms of his hands with feigned frivolity. "I heard you had a rough trip and I'm afraid I can't put you up for the evening, but I may be able to help you take a load off."

Ron rushed to take the suitcase and usher the stranger inside, holding the door and waving with his now empty, gun-favoring hand. The visitor frowned with a flash in his brown eyes and entered. The air was still severe, but Ron now felt more in control.

Inside, he offered the stranger the rest of the coffee while John played along and stayed calm. The boy played with a set of Duplos while Ron set his Beretta on the kitchen counter. He asked the visitor to lay his pork pie alongside on the table. The man agreed, setting the hat on the surface with the unmistakable clunk of metal on Formica.

The two exchanged stares showing dominance, bewilderment, reticence, or a combination of the three. Ron didn't dare lower his gaze while gesturing a left hand toward the living room and giving a nod to the sheet-wrapped call girl. He figured the visitor was just a lackey on a job. A little benefit of the doubt could spare them both from inflicting immediate violence on each other. The visitor returned a nod, easing the almost tacit tension a fraction to take care of more pressing problems.

Ron went to John, sat on the floor, and tried to keep the boy distracted with the Lego-like blocks as the man knelt down near the couch and unzipped the suitcase. Ron was relieved with the lack of noise made.

The bald muscle picked up the dead call-girl with a slow grace like a father trying not to wake a child. When John set down his Duplos and stepped toward the scene, both men tensed.

"*Por favor, señor. A dónde la llevas?*" John asked. "Where are you taking her?"

The muscle put his hand toward the boy, hesitating for a moment with Ron as a shadow. He glanced at Ron with palms up, continuing to pat the boy's head after meeting the father's death gaze with a submissive nod.

"I'm afraid *la señorita* is dead," he said. "I am here to take her for burial. Her family wants to keep it private."

John blinked and nodded, returning to his blocks. The bald lackey finished zipping the call girl inside the bag as Ron let out a breath and kept a close watch.

The man cleaned any bodily fluids from the floor and disposed of them in a Ziploc bag, which was then put in a side pocket near the dead call girl. Ron closed the distance between himself and his Beretta.

As the man watched, Ron took the visitor's revolver, hidden underneath the pork pie hat. He emptied the bullets from its cylinder barrel and then released the magazine from his Beretta while pointing both toward the wall. The unwelcome visitor kept a healthy distance from John as Ron put the revolver bullets in a separate Ziploc bag and kept the Beretta's ammo on the counter.

Ron removed the chambered bullet from his Beretta for an extra show of so-called good faith. He then offered the empty revolver and bullets to the hired goon and nodded to the door.

The man went to Ron, took his pork pie hat, stuffed the revolver and bullets in separate pockets, and then collected the roller board suitcase containing the deceased call girl and incriminating DNA evidence. He had the courtesy to give salutations with his hat at the door, only donning it after leaving.

As John continued with his Duplos, Ron reloaded the Beretta, turning the safety off before returning it to his waistband, hidden under his button down. As he and John sang "Apples and Bananas," he cracked four eggs over canola oil in a pan and made toast. After adding some *jamón y queso* to the eggs, he thought more about what he ought to do while he ate for the first time in over half a day.

John got butter and jam from the fridge and joined him, mimicking a stern face. At least he did so until Ron grinned and returned a goofy if forced look. Events needed explaining, which he expected somewhat at the meeting later with Carey's captives. Lack of control conspired to put him out of his element.

* * *

El Castillo San Felipe del Morro was just visible through the patio doors of her boss's penthouse. The phallic profile of the 16th-century citadel lighthouse barely stood out in the vast distance disconnecting the tourist destination from the swarm of early afternoon crowds of San Juan. Teenage tourists were no doubt bursting with smiles as they meandered around the U.S. Navy-built tower.

La soldado had to hide a grim smile while she readied herself to listen to the boss. She prepared to return only curt nods to show the tightly-wound weapon she had become. Dressed in military fatigues that didn't manage to hide her well-toned physique, she declined a joint and kept her light brown eyes trained straight ahead. Two topless waitresses offered Cohibas, rum, and other refreshments to associates and soldiers.

She wondered to herself whether the sloppy offerings were to compensate for something or geared to provoke her. The boss, Luis Fernando, smiled, and she interpreted the so-called hospitality was due to a little of both. Luis wouldn't have looked so amused if he could see the imagery in her head of a cocktail spear jutting through his puffy face.

When an ill-informed sycophant slapped the tight curve of *la soldado's* behind, it gave her an excuse for a welcome release of steam. The tilted baseball cap and sleeveless football jersey the *sangano* wore showed he wasn't high on the food chain, which made the release easy.

Before the guy could turn a feigned blush into a cocksure grin underneath his scant mustache, *la soldado* jabbed beneath his Adam's apple with barely nonlethal force radiating from her left fist. With her right hand, she grabbed his Cuba Libre before it could join him on the floor. She slammed the rum down her throat and took the lime wedge in her front teeth. A cocktail spear flexed between her index finger and her thumb as Luis's claps could be heard over any gasps of surprise.

To *la soldado*, three equally-fit men, his new head of security Jimmy Ocasio, an official-looking *tipo* in a navy blue suit, and assorted waitresses and thugs, Luis told everyone to take a seat. He stubbed out his cigar and had one of the *señoritas* take his rum. Two underlings, dressed similar to the man *la soldado* had just dropped, took their comrade outside of the room only to return and take a place along the wall.

Luis cleared his throat and ran a hand through his slicked-back ebony hair. *El patrón* straightened his tan sport coat as his head remained above those gathered for commands, self-interest, or both. The prospect of money and leverage kept *la soldado* as captive as everyone else.

She listened as Luis pontificated on US mainland-needed power to reign in Puerto Rican independence. *Gringos* needed locals to assist when it came to policing the police and deals with drugs and drug manufacturers. The well-coiffed man in the suit nodded along as if a conductor to keep the tempo.

Some regulars were taken aback by the semblance of an olive branch toward the US mainland. *La soldado* read between the lines. The FBI was, for the most part, geared to playing along with DEA *putos* to bust the token lower-level horse and candycaine dealers. Luis was expanding his business with those legally selling and producing opiates and all manner of medication.

Disruption of the illicit economy was a factor Luis couldn't let happen outright. His reputation as a boss protected him from straight-up prosecution, but he had to keep appearances. This echoed her suspicion he'd throw any *Boricua* beneath him for a leg up with the right *gringo*. Luis announced that a Texas-based pharmaceutical manufacturer, the Shelling-Polk Company, was the needed connection.

Cooperation with drug dealers with legitimacy was the only way to go in the long term, especially if a *narco* could befriend someone on the US mainland. If pharmaceutical companies could launder money, Luis could become the local gatekeeper.

"*Un mano lava el otro,*" Luis said. One hand washes the other.

La soldado revisited in her mind yesterday's tasks in a patch of thick foliage off of the highway. Killing the *gringo* would have put down a potential witness, and Luis had ordered her to kill Ron Riley after chatter that a snitch was on the move with law enforcement.

The score was clear enough for anyone paying attention, and *la soldado* knew her role was transitory at best, if well-paid. Luis was happy to flash his ego and he knew better than to hit on her. Did he know his usefulness was fleeting as well if he lacked loyalty with his team?

"Preguntas?" Luis asked at the end of his speech, not seeking to clarify anything.

Luis also needed to court FBI middle managers and their assets to send a message to mollify US mainland powers. Hence *el tipo* in the suit. She was pretty sure her services would no longer be sought had she killed the FBI agent that day, so any ultimate failure to kill yesterday mattered less.

As the other men in the room grabbed more rum or waitresses who looked to provide other services, Luis, the suit, and Jimmy Ocasio met in a corner of the room. Clusters of authority and pawns hinted at hierarchy around the room. *La soldado* focused on the hunt.

The three at the head of the pack held cocktail glasses with whiskey or rum on the rocks. Overheard banter clued her to the fact that the suit was one of the FBI looking for favors. He definitely noticed when she waved her firm behind, wrapped in fatigues. *La soldado* made a point of saying *hola.*

"Rodriguo de Salinas. *Mucho gusto,"* the suit said with a nod after she'd introduced herself. The suit implied he was looking forward to working with Señor Fernando to help clean up the island territory for tourists, business, and residents.

Luis quickly asked *la soldado* to give him a kiss on the cheek before hurrying her along. The boss didn't stray from diminutive dealings with her. He wanted to make plans that may or may not involve her making more money. He urged her to let the men conduct business, inflaming her desire to kill him when the time was right. She took out her frustration along the walk back to her flat in Rio Piedras.

An aggressive cat-caller took up her trail, which she allowed in hopes he'd be stupid enough to follow. At the safe house on Calle Azucena, she let him in. His mouth was wide open when she slunk out of the fatigues with nothing underneath but her boyshort panties. He closed the distance between them, misreading her seduction as submission.

When he grabbed her breast, called her *una puta,* and tried to dig his teeth into her still-healing shoulder, he made an almost fatal mistake. Bright red anger flushed *la soldado's* caramel cheeks. She penetrated him with a knife, pushed him to the ground, and kicked him in the *cojones* to keep it real.

6

Killer Queen

From his derelict quarters down the street from the lethal lady he had put under surveillance, Agent Roberto Lopez resumed his stakeout from a small window a while after waking from exhaustion. Within minutes, he saw her lure a man from the street to her quarters, waving her hips with the fluidity of a praying mantis on the hunt.

Lopez winced when he witnessed the idiot's aggression, expecting much more than self-defense from the gamine gunwoman. The lethal beauty transfixed his view. He still wavered between being wary, serving FBI interests, and getting turned on.

From her tiny porch, she appeared ravished after a short interlude, wiping the blood off her hands on a towel before she whisked her dark brown locks into a ponytail. The sporty breasts clinging under a tank top rose and fell with measured calm as the mid-afternoon sun shined down. After lighting a joint, she fished in camouflage shorts for a burner phone and dialed.

Within ten minutes of the call, sweat dripped down Agent

Lopez's brow as he watched the man with the pork pie hat and ebony skin approach the front door of the building where she stayed. She met the ebony-skinned man downstairs, passing over a man with a bleeding wound on his belly. With no apparent exchange of words with the *mujer*, pork pie slung the cat-caller across his shoulders.

La soldado wasn't in charge, as her digs were too spartan. She was no doubt an important player due to her handiness with knives and automatics. Lopez wanted to focus on her, but duty called him to follow clues as they happened.

Lopez descended the stairs of his flat in that instant. He followed the men to the Centro Médico de Puerto Rico a few blocks away, still in Río Piedras. He wondered where the trail of blood ultimately led.

Pork pie hat did his job effectively and didn't ask for any comforts. The worker bee was seen more than once to take care of the dirty work. He dropped the bleeding cat-caller outside of the Centro Médico before lighting a cigarette and moving on to the next job.

If anyone was a useful tool who didn't have aspirations, it was the ebony-skinned man with the pork pie hat. Lopez made it a point to follow the muscle. He almost envied the ability to follow orders without question. If pork pie had any qualms of conscience, it didn't interrupt the mission.

* * *

Carey woke up with the left side of her face against a cool floor contrasting with the tropical air surrounding her body. From the lack of light and cold stone, she figured she was in a basement.

She could wriggle her hips, but couldn't spread her ankles, linked together with a frayed rope. The outside of her thighs brushed sandy dirt that scraped from there up to her hips. She was pleased that her captors at least left her boyshorts and button-down top on. The air cooled with the pace she assumed was the approach of evening.

Her thoughts shifted to yesterday with her son's innocent laugh and Ron's warning from a payphone. After their toddler's bedtime routine, the next thing she remembered was masked thugs pushing past her greeting at the door. They'd muffled any cries for help, snapped a photo with her cell phone, and injected her with a shot of knockout juice.

The click-clack of boots on a stairway interrupted her thoughts of past events. A gloved hand put a rag reeking of ammonia beneath her nose.

Within seconds, green eyes peering over a sandy mustache and matching goatee met her fast-adjusting hazel irises. With breath smelling a bit less rancid than the smelling salts, he addressed her in a southern mainland dialect of English she'd heard as a kid while watching episodes of "Dallas."

In his twang, the putz introduced himself as someone representing a drug manufacturer from "the 'Lone Star State,' back in the *real* America." He told her to just call him Russ.

"Well, you are more comfortable than most, aren't ya?" he asked before spitting a wad of Skoal on the ground. "Hey Pablo, get her up, will ya?"

An ebony-skinned man with a pork pie hat and dour features crouched and picked her up with the ease of a wrestler and the gumption of an overexcited toddler.

The *gringo*-in-charge rattled in his offbeat English that he'd have preferred to screw her rather than leave her alone. He nevertheless liked seeing her tied up. He continued with commands and commentary in poorly-accented Spanish to thugs. In the dim light, she could tell one had a fairer complexion and two others were slightly lighter than "Pablo."

Although Carey was still learning the language and a bit doped, she managed to pick up hints of whatever was in store for her. Her abduction had come at the command of a local *narco*, but the drugstore cowboy figured ransom for her would be worth more in information than dollars. Her captors were hoping to make Ron their puppet, to tattle on opposition to drug dealers, both legitimized and not.

Whether corrupt *Boricuas* or *gringos* wanted a piece, she knew her husband would make them think they had him until he could get her safe. Ron proved dangerous when goons backed him into a corner. She expected corpses in her future, likely from the *pendejos* around her.

The *gringo's* gaggle of men laughed, save for the man in the hat, when the small-handed man in charge joked about her "*tetas.*" Her hazel eyes were met with lecherous tongues and batting eyes from caramel-skinned and lighter-toned faces alike until they ascended the stairs.

The only one that remained was the man with the pork pie hat. He led her up with a gentle touch and offered her water, which she drank. He also offered her a tortilla and a bucket to relieve herself before returning her to the floor.

Carey read a sense of ambivalence in his eyes after she was returned to her prostrate position on the ground. Pork pie hat produced a switchblade and cut a canvas bag, draping it over Carey as a blanket before he ascended to join the rest.

7

Meeting of the Minds

Ron walked with John the couple blocks to the *señora* with whom Carey had been friendly. His son led the way. At a small, yellow-hued trailer set a ways back from the sea, he knocked on a small door. He shifted from foot to foot to calm his nerves about leaving John under someone else's temporary care while dealing with the empowered thugs who'd abducted his wife.

What Ron imagined would be a serious and awkward introduction started out with a shriek of delight. It was jarring despite hospitable intent.

Between John's dimples, a wide grin formed when a woman aged between five and six decades, with streaks of gray in her curly chestnut hair, flashed her jagged teeth and giggled. The energy between the woman and her son soothed the scene. When she gestured the boys inside, Ron forced a smile in return.

The rapid, automatic-fire pace of Spanish from the lady did little to put him in his comfort zone. At least her tenor seemed joyful.

"*Lo siento, más lento por favor,*" Ron said, lines of worry creasing from his eyes. More slowly, please. The stubble on his face and streaks of gray in his unwashed mane made him look older.

"Ehhh, okay," the lady said. "English is okay? I am called Margarita. You are Papa Ron, yes?"

"*Sí*. and you know my son, John, and his mother, my wife, Carey, *sí?*" Ron asked, still standing in the doorway with a forced smile.

"*Sí*, John is good boy, Señor Riley. Your wife is good mother. Can I help you with something?"

When Ron let his grip on his son soften, the boy ran into Margarita's arms to be embraced in a full hug. A preemptive unease met an ounce of calm. He usually found it naïve to trust so completely in someone based on instinct, but Carey's impression and John's apparent affection were enough to cast off lingering doubts.

The stout, caramel-skinned woman beckoned him inside. John made himself comfortable on a tan mini futon next to a stack of paperback novels on a homemade bookshelf.

She held up a juice pitcher from the small fridge and waited for Ron to give a nod of approval before pouring the contents into a tiny coffee mug and offering it to the smiling John.

Margarita offered a beer to Ron, which he declined before she poured chicory-scented brew for herself from a coffee carafe taken from a hot plate. She gestured for Ron to sit at the futon as she took a small folding chair from the tiny kitchenette.

The hospitality helped Ron relax, but not enough to share a complete description of the day's events. In broken, still developing Spanish, along with hand gestures and enunciated English, he got his point across.

He told Margarita that he had to take care of recent affairs concerning Carey and himself. Carey considered her a friend and he asked if she could watch John and keep him safe for a while, perhaps through the evening.

The immediate smile on Margarita's face, as well as the genuineness of her brown-eyed gaze, were enough evidence to allow John to stay under her care. He figured it was better to leave him with her than juggle either leaving a four-year-old to himself or within shouting distance of guys whose business included disposing of dead call-girls.

"No hay problemas," Margarita replied with a warm grin, continuing with a quick search of the cabinets in the kitchenette. As she started water to a boil on the hot plate where the coffee had been, she brought out dry black beans and ham. Ron leaned toward John on the futon.

John was shuffling a deck of cards by putting all fifty-two on the ground beneath him and mixing them. He then placed five cards in front of him and five cards on the other side of the pile, all faced down. After crossing his legs in a pretzel-shape, he informed Ron of what he was doing.

"Margarita plays cards like Aunt Peggy," he said. "This game's called Go Fish."

Ron pecked John on the forehead and told him to be good. He returned his first real smile for the day before taking Margarita's hands in the kitchenette. He exchanged goodbyes in Spanish before leaving.

"Aunt Peggy, I've come to realize I'm never alone," Ron muttered to himself, addressing the spirit of the woman who had raised him before he headed for college over a decade ago. Aunt Peggy was the only person he missed from the Chicago suburbs.

After blinking back a tear, he caught a cab to meet with his wife's abductors at the destination scribed on a note. Memories of bittersweet times over whiskey and cards with his aunt mixed with thoughts of keeping his current family alive. He felt his son was safe. A sense of tranquility otherwise escaped him.

* * *

The Starbucks in Río Piedras was too *yuppie* for many of the locals, save government bureaucrats, students at the local campus of the Universidad de Puerto Rico, and tourist guides. The espressos and café at the shop on Plaza Olmedo were okay but wasn't anything homemade Bustelo could beat.

Along the way to Starbucks, Agent Roberto Lopez had followed pork pie for a visit to a row house, where all the blinds were conveniently drawn. Pork pie exited within an hour after changing a shirt that had been streaked with blood from his errand for *la soldado*. A man wearing a cowboy hat joined pork pie for the coffee trip, and the two now took a seat on the patio.

Lopez had managed to pick up a pair of chinos and a navy blue *guayabera* along the way. He felt like a dork wearing them, but they helped him blend in with the corporate coffee shop crowd.

After ordering an espresso straight up, Lopez sat indoors by a window open to the view. He opened a crime novel he'd picked up at a used bookstore stall. He could hear the two outside conversing.

Cowboy hat seemed agitated, wondering out loud in poorly-accented Spanish if a *gringo* he wanted to use as a patsy would show up. He doubted the muscular, pork pie-hatted man had made enough of an impression, whether his local help had been hard enough.

"He's more smart than he look," pork pie said in better-accented English. "He more interested in making deals and keeping his *hijo* safe than showing me his *cojones*."

"It's easier to deal with a fella who's not itchin' to shoot off his gun," the cowboy responded in kind. "I'll grant you that, but this prick better know I'm serious as the business end of a .45. Well look 'ere, we got ourselves our man, my jigaboo, beaner friend."

Lopez recognized the campy Texan accent. The drugstore cowboy sounded like pharmaceutical investors he'd heard on the news. He wondered why home office hadn't yet called on a full operation yet, but he didn't expect much diligence against investors from the US mainland. He wondered what the hell the cowboy was talking about.

With a chance glance out of the window, beyond the patio, he saw a familiar, albeit scruffier face. The *gringo* from the dance with the automatic, which had set in motion Lopez' clandestine operations, walked up. The recognizable rogue took a seat with the two.

Lopez returned his nose to his crime novel, nervous he'd be recognized but pleased that his surveillance was unraveling a pattern. The back and forth put him too much on edge to concentrate on his book. Based on his recent memories from the shadows of a shot-up Dodge sedan in the dense foliage along the highway, it was quite obvious that the pharma cowboy was underestimating the character with whom he was dealing.

Lopez figured the road to restoring a sense of repose would

require retribution toward rascals ripping apart the law from the inside. "Fighting the power" was as American as capitalism, after all. He realized *el gringo* could become an unlikely ally.

* * *

North of Rio Piedras, in the same mid-rise structure containing Luis Fernando's penthouse, *la soldado* was bored with playing bodyguard. It wasn't just that, but the FBI prick, Rodriguo de Salinas, mistook her interest in power players as flirtation. She would let him fantasize so she could listen in on the conversation between him and a friendly local *narco*. Her annoyance took a back seat when she had to work her assets.

"Why not kill Lopez?" Luis asked in a conference room sealed off from any view of El Castillo San Felipe del Morro. Though the phallic symbol of the tower was unseen, dominance and misplaced machismo pervaded the quarters. "We could easily pass it off as collateral damage between drug gangs."

Assistant Special Agent-in-Charge de Salinas cocked his head to the side, breaking away from a glance at *la soldado's* hips to focus condescending bemusement at the local gatekeeper, Luis. He gave the praying mantis soldier a wink before addressing his host. His calm was ever present.

"We have several assets in play, Señor Fernando," he said, exhaling a cloud of smoke from a blunt. "Agent Lopez is loyal to duty and still takes orders from me. He could be useful as long as he doesn't link me with you and our Shelling-Polk cowboy friend. We'll take him out and the *gringo* he abducted when they're no longer useful."

Luis ran a finger under his nose and nodded more quickly

than the conventions of casual conversation. The boss's apprehension was apparent, and the coke didn't help.

"So we take a risk?" the *narco* said.

"It's manageable with a greater reward," the wayward FBI agent said. "Trust me. Now, why not enjoy the fruits of our labor?"

De Salinas lurched toward *la soldado* before Luis directed one of his best-earning call-girls to make a move. Luis and his soldier were both pleased when the federal agent chose the barely legal gal for release.

When de Salinas and the working girl meandered off to a private room, Luis convened in a corner of the conference room with his new head of security, Jimmy Ocasio and *la soldado.* The boss laid down the way events should actually come to pass. He focused on Ocasio, appearing almost dismissive of *la soldado* as she listened.

Ocasio was to keep an eye on de Salinas but otherwise maintain his primary duties guarding Luis. The man nodded, but his heart didn't seem to beat with any sense of urgency. The indifference to duty didn't seem to bother the boss.

La soldado was to take this Agent Lopez from his surveillance of her to captivity at Luis's command. She had enjoyed luring the agent with a dance of seduction during his so-called stakeout, and would gladly make him an asset.

She admired the man's skill with a .45, so she left it up to her whims and whatever happened in the field as to whether she turned him over to Luis. Lopez was to become leverage. He was well-trained and moderately handsome, but handier as a tool for now.

Lopez could become her tool if events played out that way There were other elements at play for *la soldado.* None included strong allegiance to Luis Fernando. There was the question of money, but loyalty for payment was tenuous at best.

8

Help a Brother Out

Ron awoke about an hour after the sun rose and wandered to the kitchen to find John standing on his tiptoes to reach the cereal cabinet. He crouched down and snuck up behind his son. There wasn't a noise in the muggy air except for the tick of the clock. When he was within a foot of John, the boy reacted in a split second.

John shifted his weight, balancing his body in a squat while he turned around and lunged. Ron caught the boy's right-hand jab with a soft deflection before his son could make a punch to the groin. The four-year-old gave a defiant flash of teeth.

"I taught you well, son," Ron said. "Only some basics and you can put an Army veteran on defense."

John gave a shit-eating grin in the slim light of sun caressing the eastern horizon. His dazed eyes showed he hadn't slept well. He was no doubt adjusting to disruptions in schedule and a missing mother.

"Lucky Charms?" Ron asked, unsure of how to productively deal with the boy's or his own anxiety. It was better to stick to a routine.

"Push-ups first," John responded.

Ron gave a wary grin and got on the ground next to his son in the adjacent living room, pleased to immerse himself in exercise.

The boy did a round of fifteen push-ups and sit-ups as Ron rattled off his fifty of each. As John stretched and Ron completed his core exercises, the elder Riley thought about the events of the week.

Since meeting the pork pie-clad worker bee and his Texas-accented handler yesterday evening at a Starbucks in Rio Piedras, Ron felt the pawn among assholes looking to make money and screw everyone else.

Per usual, he would have told the dicks in charge to shove it and do whatever was physically necessary to escape the situation and kick some shitbags out of rotation. But since starting a life with Carey and becoming a father, his *modus operandi* had changed.

He decided to play ball until he could make a move.

Per the prick with the cheesy Texan accent, Ron Riley was to do what he could to monitor *Boricua* dissent against the U.S. mainland business, in particular, big pharma. He was to report any stray gossip about a heroin and cocaine godfather called Luis Fernando. Ron remembered the *narco*'s name as uttered from a woman dying in his living room the day before.

Any disobedience would put Carey at risk. The threats and conspiracy sounded like something out of a pulp novel or documentary challenging the War on Drugs.

Ron was to keep tending bar at El Rococo, show up to the occasional protest and report on those he saw, and give any information to a roster of police friendly to the Shelling-Polk Corporation, the pharmaceutical maker the drugstore cowboy represented. If all went well, Carey and he would be free to reunite, allegedly.

The wannabe cowboy had held a paring knife to his thumb as he had said Ron's cooperation was "much appreciated." Working for the ass was the last thing Ron wanted to do. He wanted to kick the guy's latte on his pants and plug him with the Beretta.

Thoughts of Carey and John reigned him in. That, and he'd been told to leave his pistol at home by the same pork pie-hatted muscle who had been eyeing him throughout the entire back and forth. At the end of the meeting, they gave him a Motorola burner to keep in touch.

Back in the present, with John again reaching toward the cereal cabinet, Ron stopped his thoughts to help out. He poured boxed milk in John's Lucky Charms before peeling an orange and putting it beside the boy. He then brewed coffee and poured himself a bowl of sugary goodness. His son's smiles gave him some hope.

Ron had checked in with his pal, FBI Agent Russo, relaying most of the information from the meeting at Starbucks. Russo's attentive ear and Margarita's willingness to watch John during the day gave him optimism about his family's safety. Once he achieved that, he'd look for the right moment to make these bastards pay. If he could clean up affairs for the locals, all the better.

After a shower for him and John, he packed the boy a peanut butter sandwich and took him to Margarita's. He kept his Beretta in his back waistband, no round chambered, concealed under a loose-fitting tropical button down. Ron didn't want to make any locals nervous on the bus to his job at El Rococo.

At least his son was safe, and the weather was nice.

* * *

The early morning in bed was rendered cooler than the air from an overworked air conditioner in early spring Miami heat. When Matt Russo sought nookie at dawn, he found his wife, Clara, was not in the mood. She told him he smelled before yanking the covers toward her side of the mattress.

Instead of a dalliance with his wife, while she was only in undergarments and a T-shirt, she took the next hour to shower and don a designer black pantsuit with red stiletto heels. She looked with disdain down to him as he took his time, still in bed.

Still clad in plaid boxers and a white T-shirt, he cupped his package with a feeble attempt at protection at seeing her taut lips and the heavy mascara framing her icy eyes. Her black leather business purse was slung like a chambered M16.

"What's up honey?" he said.

Russo had, according to his wife, mumbled something in his sleep about off-hours research into his old buddy Ron's troubles in Puerto Rico. That, and he had let a few whiskey-scented comments slip about a ball-strangling desk career and an ice queen wife.

The veins on Clara's graceful neck showed she was *not* in the mood for jokes. He was too sleepy for a perfect answer and too intelligent to try charm. He still offered self-deprecation and a stupid grin.

"Men are stupid when they're awake, dear," he said. "We can't measure up when we're asleep."

"Your skills might be slipping with the boredom of the desk and a bitchy wife," Clara responded. "I expect more subtlety from someone who can keep guard over government secrets."

With offers to treat her and Zoe out for breakfast rebuffed, Russo took out the trash and cleaned the kitchen as his two ladies got ready for their days. Clara dodged a kiss to the cheek before he bent down to get a hug from his daughter. The two left in the Saturn Aura hybrid much earlier than they needed, leaving Matt Russo to his own devices.

After frying up some eggs and cheese and brewing some instant coffee because Mr. Coffee was on the fritz, he breakfasted on the patio of their Coconut Grove condo. Still in his boxers and T-shirt, he lit a cigarette before sipping Sanka. The "coffee" sucked, but the smoke made up for it. He gave brief consideration to the pint of Seagrams whiskey he had stashed but pushed total self-destruction from his thoughts. He supposed it was Zoe's hug that kept him in check.

Realizing Clara had reason to be upset, Russo's thoughts wandered back to Ron Riley. He shoveled fat and protein with a hot sauce assist into his mouth with the efficiency of a zipped-up, second generation Roomba.

He thought about what he had found on local blogs about a bullet-ridden Dodge outside San Juan. FBI intranet hinted to Russo the feelings held by any jaded federal agent about law enforcement leaders with unearned authority. Assistant Special Agent-in-Charge Rodriguo de Salinas was either too ambitious about looking good or was covering his tracks. Russo suspected the latter.

After he finished his eggs, he decided to down another "coffee" while he thought about news of Carey's abduction and Ron's observations about the hostage holder with a campy Texas accent. He decided against another cigarette as his thoughts smoldered.

The dead call-girl and kidnapped Carey were enough to

alarm Russo, but Ron's observations of the reappearing muscle, the one with a pork pie hat joining one with a cowboy hat outside of a Puerto Rican Starbucks ignited contemplation of a conspiracy. Ron had told him the cowboy wanted reports on island insurgents and rebels to earn Carey's release.

An interesting news item that pinged on his Toshiba described a representative of the Houston-based Shelling-Polk Corporation, Russell Thurgood. The cowboy-hatted "Russ" Thurgood was addressing cooperation between locals and US mainland officials with pharmaceutical production on the island. A shootout outside San Juan was brought up by a quickly-quieted reporter before the drugstore cowboy speculated that, "radical elements often want to politicize local gang and drug violence for their cause."

Russo compared video footage of Russell Thurgood with Ron's description from the evening before. The connection was getting clearer. With plans for more side research into the Shelling-Polk Corporation, he didn't expect to find a sterling reputation.

Russo's side mission for his friend was more visceral than the busy-work of his job, signing off on official responses to more nuanced intelligence briefings. Still, his status as Supervisory Special Agent called for a sober, mostly interested presence at work. Plus, if he got fired, his wife would kill him.

Agent Russo shivered off his theories while cleaning up breakfast. In an instant, he downed his Sanka and went to relieve himself. He donned his shirt, tie, and suit coat after washing his face and clearing intrigue from his mind. It was a half hour until he had to clock in at the FBI Miami office, and he needed to put himself together for work. He got in his Ford Taurus and hit the highway.

9

Turn up the Heat

Carey flexed her legs per usual after waking, realizing they were no longer bound. The restraints remaining on her wrists, the smell of the dank basement, and the thought that her life was in the hands of unsocial thugs pushed away optimism. The constant surveillance was the harshest nemesis.

She was always under watch, even when relieving herself in a bucket. The ebony-skinned man in the pork pie hat was present today to help her get to the bucket in time. At least he turned around and faced the wall without the need for her to ask. Despite the confinement, it was the closest feeling she'd attained that involved trust.

"Cómo se llamas?" Carey asked after finishing.

"I am called Pablo, *señora,*" said the ebony-skinned man with the pork pie hat. "You are called Carey, *sí?*"

She nodded, pleading with a pitiful look with hazel eyes. Pablo squeezed her arm while leading her to a cot.

"Agua?" he asked, met with her nod.

After Carey received a cool drink, Pablo gave her a tortilla and told her in Spanish that everything would be over soon enough. From what she could understand, his boss would get what he needed and then Carey and her family would no longer be useful as captives.

She hoped the ominous message was more due to meaning lost in translation than to how forces on the ground stood. Still, she prepared herself for the worst. The boss's twangy accent rattled in her skull as she brought her knees to her chest. Carey could still feel Pablo's eyes on her, so she tried to distract both him and her on a different tack.

Her bound hands reached from the crimson locks atop her head and ran a trail, as best she could manage, past the dimples on her cheeks, past the slender alabaster neck, to the cleft peeking out of her button-down shirt. She moaned in a sound that was part fatigue and part sensuality born out of ennui.

She gave off an air of innocence, yet disdain that seduced men fleeing from adolescent monotony or other self-enforced mediocrity. It was a trick she'd learned to flaunt as a stripper in the Chicago suburbs. Using the terms of her former co-workers, she knew how to "pump a guy up;" make him see himself as the captain of the football team when he was only as powerful as the water boy.

Pablo cleared his throat as she heard footsteps in the room, coming toward her. She managed to undo another button to her shirt, limiting her vision to a winning an ally. She was just over thirty-two but knew how to make a man and the occasional woman blush. Every captor was looking for fun with a Lolita.

"Well damn, honey." said a campy, Texas-accented voice belonging to Russ, the boss. "You don't need to put on such a fine show for little ol' me."

Carey realized the footsteps originated from the stairs but

were closing in on her. Her mouth suddenly became dry at the conclusion. She clammed up as her captor made himself known. The lushness of her chest and hips suddenly grew slack.

"Sorry to disappoint you, toots," the drugstore cowboy said. "I can see you got the goods, but I pay *chicas* from the *barrio* a lot less for services my wife never heard of. I haven't taken a girl against her will since Yale. But what do you say, Pedro? You willing to enjoy some goods for a little pay cut? Might do you good."

Pablo didn't correct the boss on the name. He sighed and groaned as if trying to make up his mind.

"God damn it, Pedro," he said. "You beaners told our Muslim president you want to be in the States. Act like it! Don't look a gift horse in the mouth."

The relative coolness of the basement dropped several degrees until Pablo cleared his throat again. Carey held her breath. She realized her chest was sticking out more when she felt the *gringo*-in-charge's hand slap her behind. With a flash of heat behind her ears, she bit her tongue instead of adding anger to the air.

"I am not sure-" Pablo muttered before being interrupted.

Carey blushed as the drugstore cowboy let out a laugh.

"Well, Pedro, seeing as how I don't give a damn about your sense of morality and don't wanna pay a beaner more than I oughta, I suggest you enjoy the fruits of labor. I'll send one of my American boys to clean up and take a picture of our *chica* here when you're done with her. Might serve to motivate her husband to 'toe the line.'"

"Yeah, okay, boss" Pablo responded in a seemingly resigned voice.

Carey loathed the way the conversation was going, but if the previous days taught her anything, it was that paradise wasn't as much a way out as a mirage to hide the ugliness of the world. She listened to steps ascend. Her spirit felt like it was drowning as the boss left.

It was then that she hoped for a throw ring for safety.

"*Qué pasa*, Pablo?" she said.

"*Lo siento, señora*," he responded. "The boss is full of *mierda*. I must ask that we make it look like he is in charge."

Her hazel eyes met Pablo's brown, asking with hope for what he had in mind.

After a whisper to her ear about setting a ruse for the *pendejo*-in-charge, she nodded before he unclasped her hands and let her set the scene. Like when she had been relieving herself, he turned around.

Carey was happy she didn't have to debase herself to gain leverage.

When another henchman, descended the stairs a short time later, he found a sweaty Carey collapsed on the floor with a torn top, apparently unconscious. Pablo was in a corner wiping his hands and forehead with a piece of her shirt.

It was a good setup for anyone not playing on the fly. The tables were about to turn.

* * *

La soldado arched her back and flexed her biceps and calves. The feeling returned to her arms as the afternoon rolled around like a satisfied lover casually kissing her before going to make a sandwich. Knowing she was under watch, she put on a sensuous show for her soon-to-be asset. After donning boyshorts and a sports bra she took a shot of *ron blanco* in her mug before putting some instant Café Bustelo with a pint of water in a saucepan atop a hot plate.

She decided to take a moment for herself on her small balcony. She was unsure if it was in her best interest to be tasked with keeping an eye on both the *gringo* and the Fed whom she'd failed earlier in the week to kill. Luis gave her money, and Assistant Special Agent-in-Charge de Salinas was smitten. So that was what ultimately counted.

The pork pie-wearing *negro* had delivered a gray pencil skirt for her uniform, which currently hung on a chair inside. Her cargo fatigues were hanging on the railing outside, the grime rinsed off in the previous night's rain shower. In her panties, she sipped the instant coffee, having grabbed a banana and a piece of *pan de Mallorca* for a small breakfast.

The automatic rifle cadence of sandpipers in the background interrupted her thoughts as she chewed her food. She downed her coffee and went inside to use the water closet before donning the skirt, a light blue, V-neck, sleeveless blouse, and flats. She then pinned her hair up with a clip and stepped downstairs to street level. Outside, she strode casually over the cobblestone sidewalk to catch the bus to Fajardo.

She smirked, realizing her follower, Agent Lopez, was likely enjoying the view.

* * *

Agent Roberto Lopez was enjoying his stakeout of *la soldado* despite frustrations. He had checked in with FBI headquarters and reported what he saw.

His surveillance linked clandestine local drug operations

with a presence from the US mainland. The chicanery included cooperation with municipal police, the subtle sexual dance of his *femme fatale,* and more blatantly spilled blood.

Assistant Special Agent-in-Charge de Salinas had ordered him to keep an eye out, follow the woman, but tread lightly when it came to US mainland connections. The most important instruction was to maintain a low profile, to report directly to de Salinas. The demand for control from his superior irked Lopez, but there wasn't much he could do about it in the present.

Lopez was happy to not have to deal with paperwork or in-office debriefings. His motives weren't all professional nor solely out of a sense of official justice. The tough, knife-toting *mujer* excited him.

He was tired of living off of pocket change and only entertaining himself with gossip rags and caffeine when not enjoying the view across the street. The boss had given him permission to engage on the down-low.

His surveillance of the ebony-skinned man with the pork pie hat was also bringing a theory of events full circle. The dark-skinned muscle had accompanied a boss figure with a Texas-like accent the other day before they both sat down with the *gringo* who had started all his troubles and suspicions.

Everyone seemed to be threaded together in a web of deception, death, and desire. Lopez figured a way to take control was to get in touch with *la soldado*. Either her, the *gringo*, or pork pie were his ticket to understanding events. She interested him the most.

Following the *femme fatale*, Lopez got on the bus to Fajardo. He sat in the back as he glanced on occasion above recently-acquired sunglasses at the petite, deadly, *mujer*. It had only been a few years since his education at the University of Puerto Rico and his stint at Quantico to train for the FBI, and *la soldado* had been the first woman to catch his attention since a few college girls. The fact that she'd fired automatic rounds at him was more cause for excitement than worry.

Her dark locks were pinned up in a clip, but a stray tendril strayed down her strong neck to the deadly muscles of her upper shoulders, Her attention seemed diverted out the window, so Agent Lopez trailed the line to the sporty curve of her breasts and the adjacent sinewy bicep muscles. He considered himself quick enough to divert his attention to his used crime novel when she gave him a glance.

He briefly felt the shame of an altar boy while having impure thoughts in the repressing spirit of his time at a Catholic high school. With the realization that the stakes were bigger, he nodded off the streak of sweat rolling down his cheek to ready himself for what he needed to do.

Agent Lopez stood when *la soldado* got off her bus seat at Fajardo. When she departed, he departed. Keeping what he assumed was a safe distance, he followed her to an alley off of the main road. He reassured himself that he could still see the sinews of her sensuous silhouette. She appeared to turn right, and he followed.

At the end of the alley, Lopez peered to the right and saw El Rococo bar across the street. He tensed when a large shadow moved toward the periphery of his view. The last complete image he saw in his head was the face of *la soldado*. The view was followed by a punch from his left. He felt himself being dragged back into the alley. The ensuing darkness was deep.

10

Around the Watering Hole

Rob Riley finished a cup of instant Bustelo before his late afternoon/early evening shift at El Rococo. The twenty-stool black Formica, wraparound bar was nothing fancy. Above it, a chalkboard adorned with Corona and Heineken stickers outlined fried specials from a short order cook in the back. Hardly anyone came for the food.

What set this watering hole apart from every dive bar in the Midwest was an unplanned sense of culture. Guitar picking flamenco-melodies and the syncopated beat of wood blocks danced in the air. Wide patio doors opened to a terrace framed with curved palm trees. The two billiards tables seemed out of place, but serious bets later in the evening could lead to occasional fist fights.

He took a few minutes to unwind until his shift serving drunks who preyed on tourists, wayward government clerks, local laborers, and giving homeless boys or girls an occasional snack from the kitchen. After a sandwich and checking his Beretta, he was ready to work and observe until his shift ended and he picked up John.

The twentysomething, daytime waitress gave him a chaste simper before saying goodbye. He returned the smile when she put her wavy ebony locks in a ponytail and tangoed her bomba-dress clad hips out the door to get her daughter from school.

While serving cans of Medalla Light to a half dozen *campesinos*, Ron understood a few whispers about *explotación* and *opiatos* along with what he translated as gossip about a *gringo* pharmaceutical firm. The Shelling-Polk Corporation was apparently not a hit, having made offers to buy farmland that low-balled the actual value while still citing the recovering economy. No one at the bar had caved to the scam, *el engaño*.

Ron kept half an ear cocked toward the *campesinos,* but conveniently missed out on conversation when it got into any areas that might cause them harm. To maintain plausible deniability with the big pharma cowboy, he moved on to serve a bank teller from Carolina a Heineken and then welcomed a half dozen *policías*. He couldn't report what he couldn't hear.

Los policías also wanted to get hints about local drug trafficking, both to prosecute it and to exploit it. Ron served them shots of Bacardi either before or after their own shifts. At least two of them were on Thurgood's list of friendlies.

It was then that Officer Carlos Velez, a Puerto Rico state police, *un uniformado*, in whom Ron confided, entered the bar. He started razing any *policía* who were due for duty and knocked over a shot that had poured for a coworker.

Carlos gave the third degree to the man, using a raised eyebrow only slightly darker than the hint of his mustache. Authority befitted him, and he didn't hide the fact that he was hoping to make sergeant within the year.

The few months of back and forth between him and Ron

started a camaraderie. Carlos showed up for work sober and stayed that way with an ear to shady avenues and those exploited by less honorable law enforcement. Ron understood the discipline and desire to help innocents stay living. It was a solid symbiosis, especially since Carlos wasn't anywhere near the list of police friendly to Shelling-Polk or Thurgood.

"*Buenas tardes*, Carlos," Ron said, popping open a Good O Kola for the man. "I need you to translate something for your friends here."

The two exchanged a wink as Ron's mind flashed to the call girl informant overdosing in his home. He decided to keep mum about it for now. Thurgood, the cowboy holding Carey hostage, likely wanted him to keep his mouth shut, too.

"I've seen a *gringo* peddling baggies to kids outside the Pueblo Supermarket west of Carolina. He was fat, like all of us from the north. He wore a shirt with flamingos and a Chicago Cubs hat over a goatee-framed face. Probably a pervert or something looking for ghetto *chicos*. He offered me a good deal for some herb, but I guess I'm too old. It sounds like a job for a few cops who could use either a bust or a score."

Carlos gave a light chuckle and relayed the disinformation in staccato Spanish, making the other *uniformados* stand at attention despite any rum. He ordered them to carry out different tasks, surveillance, note-taking, and apprehension of anyone suspicious who fit the description. His *compadre*s rushed to get to work. Ron waved them out the door as his friend nursed the Kola.

"So what's really going on, *amigo*?" said Carlos, who could have passed for a shorter, more masculine 1980s version of Jimmy Smits. "You look a little older since last week. I didn't know you were going gray. Does *tu mujercita* like it?"

After holding up his index finger to wait, Ron filled two beers for the *campesinos*, then poured a shot of rail *ron blanco* for a fella who'd just cashed a retirement check. He took his time getting back to Carlos to consider how much faith he had in the man and to collect his thoughts at the mention of Carey. He concentrated on looking cocky rather than concerned.

"Yeah, Carey's been in a rut," Ron replied, just audible above the hum of background noise. The low volume signaled to Carlos to respond in kind, to keep things on the down low and use a bit of slang the locals might not know. "Truth be told, she hasn't been home much, so-"

"Hold on," Carlos cut him off, signaling he was wise with a barely perceptible nod. "Your old lady might be mad? You want me to get the rest of the po-po on the horn?"

Ron gave a quick roll of his eyes with a slight smile. Carlos was being a dick but knew how to keep it copacetic. He was bending Russell Thurgood's rules, a risk to his wife's safety for the moment. Anyone else at the bar who'd paid attention to the two and the foreign talk had moved on.

"Pipe down, dingbat," Ron said. "I like a honey with piss and vinegar. I might be the one being somebody's bitch."

With more forced slang, Ron explained about the interaction with Russell Thurgood and his orders to keep an eye on locals opposed to business from the US mainland, in particular, Shelling-Polk. From the meeting, he learned San Juan drug kingpin Luis Fernando was in Thurgood's toolbox. The *narco* was likely looking at legal drug dealers in US pharma for a leg up. Carlos had heard rumors along the same lines but was told with more subtle hints than those Ron had received to look the other way.

Ron interrupted the back and forth to refill drinks and greet a few new customers, one of whom was a petite, fit, caramel-skinned woman in conservative dress. Her subtle, almost businesslike, beauty betrayed no warmth. He swore he felt a familiar presence about her from somewhere, making a mental note before returning to Carlos.

"We oughta keep an eye out for an ugly *gringo*," he continued. "You and I can check in about it later. Come on by the crib for a cold one sometime when you're not on the clock."

Carlos Velez nodded with a grin, giving a casual salute before heading out of El Rococo. He had to meet with his men to look for the ghosts of tourist perverts around the Pueblo Supermarket. Ron returned to the *campesinos* to freshen their drinks and pick up what he could from their colloquial Spanish.

The pretty pixie had taken a seat at the far corner of the bar and rolled a smoke. While trying to remind himself of why she might be familiar, Ron picked something up about *"un vaquero loco y torcido"* that rang a bell. Crooked, crazy cowboys were apparently all the rage these days.

After finishing with the farmers, he mixed a Cuba Libre for the banker in the middle of the bar, and the social focus shifted to where the woman was sitting.

A local cigar shop owner had entered since Ron was serving the *campesinos*. The man was known as a *pendejo* in the worst way. The poorly-maintained van dyke framing the otherwise moderately handsome, middle-aged face didn't help him escape his reputation.

The shop owner was slightly less slim than a dope fiend. He slunk up to the lady as Ron was going to get her order. He offered her a light from his Zippo, with no attempt to conceal an attempt to look down the lady's V-neck.

Cat-calls were whispered here and there upon her entrance, but the handsy cigar-seller distinguished himself from other dirtbags. Ron flushed with embarrassment on behalf of his gender when the putz snuck a kiss to her cheek and laid a hand lower, presumably toward her leg. The blush in his cheeks made it harder to stifle a laugh with the lady's response.

Cigar *culo* got an uppercut strong enough to send him to the floor. Other douchebags were about to help him off the ground until a look from the pixie told them to back off. She adjusted her V-neck as one of *la policía* who had stayed behind escorted the handsy man out of Rococo for everyone's safety. Ron polished glasses until the bar resumed the normal quiet of people looking for inebriation instead of the fire of excitement.

It was then that Ron approached the gal after she gave a flick of her wrist. She ordered a double of Bacardi Anejo after striking a match to light her smoke on her own accord. Those who had been looking averted their eyes, not paying any mind when the scent of cannabis wafted through the air. No one else was looking for an ass-kicking.

Any other men in El Rococo kept their distance. The strong gal's willingness to cut through bullshit was refreshing to Ron. She left after an ice water as the hour hand on the 1970s era clock hit ten. He watched her briefly before handing over bar duty to end his shift. He retrieved his Beretta and got to the tasks at hand.

He had to pick John up from Margarita's, take care of his adopted son, and stay mostly under the radar. His curiosity called him to stray into trouble, per what was natural, but pragmatism kept him focused on what he could do. He had to protect the most innocent and keep a half-assed eye out for locals revolting against poseurs who deserved to get screwed.

* * *

La soldado followed Ron Riley for a while after he left El Rococo. She would have enjoyed wearing a more tactical outfit than a pencil skirt and her businesslike blouse. She needed to look less like a mercenary, but still threatening enough for smarter macho guys to realize they didn't stand a chance.

She had noticed Agent Roberto Lopez watching her earlier on the bus to Fajardo. He had pretended to only be paying attention to his novel, but he definitely recognized her, as well. Per Luis's command, she had tricked him and smacked the Fed unconscious before calling the boss for backup to take him to an undisclosed location outside the capital.

When she saw Ron approach a yellowish trailer, *la soldado* ducked for cover behind a bush along the road and watched. A woman, older, brought out a preschool-aged boy. The *señora* kissed the boy on the cheek and gave Ron a hug that was meant to be friendly but only made the man blush with apparent embarrassment.

La soldado followed Ron and the boy to their home, where through a window she saw him tuck the boy in bed, retreat to the living room, and put a bit of whiskey in a coffee cup. *El gringo* then sat at a couch with a notebook, scribbling notes and sipping spirits.

She decided to get back to the FBI man who'd been following her. The Fed could be more of a problem than a guy looking out for his family. It made sense to prioritize. She called Luis on her burner to confirm the plan.

At any rate, it would probably prove easier to exploit the FBI agent's desire to live and any latent patriotism than directly take on a father watching over his son. Agent Lopez had proven a good shot, and *la soldado* was somewhat looking forward to making his acquaintance when he was unarmed. It was rare when men impressed her, even rarer when they outmaneuvered her.

11

Fight or Flight

Carey punched the other henchman in the face. It was payback for getting handsy after descending the stairs to where she and Pablo had set the scene. Within a second, she was straddling the goon, firing jabs to his face. Only Pablo's firm hand on her tense, alabaster shoulder stopped her from killing the lecherous help.

When she turned to face the ebony-skinned guard who had assisted her, the earnestness in his eyes softened her anger. When he shook his fist toward his head, she rolled her eyes and shrugged rather than admit her apprehension to hit him. He mumbled he'd have to get hurt to throw off the idea he was a party to her escape.

Pablo made it easier by caressing her shoulder and feigning an attempt to take advantage. She reacted with a punch that did more than simply leave a flushed cheek. When he managed a smile through bloodied teeth and nodded toward a narrow hopper window in the upper part of the basement north side wall, she showed she was a quick study.

The guard-turned-accomplice took a tarp from a water

pump and handed it to her after she rearranged her top to cover as much as she was able. Standing on his tiptoes, he smashed the window with the butt of his Colt revolver before getting into a crouch. With his other hand, he beckoned her to use his shoulder as a step stool.

Carey took the tarp to cover the broken glass. As she heard steps race to the stairway above, she exited the window. She ran toward an alleyway as several gunshots ripped through the air and echoed behind her. More than shouts followed her trail.

The blasts and brouhaha disturbed her, threading pangs of worry about the conscientious collaborator in her escape. Carey fled through the alley and turned left to the main thoroughfare, lit only with street lights after dusk. She slowed her step and fixed her button-down in an attempt to act as casually as she could. She wasn't wearing more than her button-down shirt and underwear but was thankful the warm climate made her outfit suitable enough for physical comfort.

Any cat-calls were met with faked coy giggles rather than customary backtalk. She would've preferred to give a bloody lip to macho men who deserved it. Still, Carey figured she'd better play diminutive a damsel in distress than be herself.

After about four blocks of laughing off attention and sticking to shadows, Carey's pulse slowed as she increased her pace along a stone passageway. The soles of her feet throbbed but worked with her muscular legs well to propel her forward.

Eventually, she found herself among couples and clusters of university students along Avenida José de Diego, having pilfered a sarong to tie around her hips. She thanked her willingness and ability to keep to the margins of attention to help her blend in. Carey figured her erstwhile captors, though nervous about her escape, also appreciated the lack of spectacle.

Thoughts of Ron and John entered Carey's head as she eventually took a seat along the wall of a bookstore closed for the evening and crossed her legs. Pedestrian traffic around her slowed as she found herself as desperate as she was when fleeing the mob in Chicago's suburbs, if not more so.

When a light-skinned tourist with a Midwestern US accent offered her change, Carey took it before adjusting herself in an alley and moving on. She wiped away a stray tear rolling down her cheek and felt overwhelmed by the need to return to her boys. She tried to will any needed sleep from her mind, but as she strayed to a beach hugging the Atlantic Ocean, exhaustion sunk in.

After her toes hit grains of sand, Carey drifted away from a group of strangers gathered around a bonfire. As the nearly half-shaded moon lighted her path, she found a few coconut palms and rested against one. Though her mind was full, the rustle of the waves and spent adrenaline allowed her mind to drift and her eyes to close.

* * *

Agent Roberto Lopez woke up on a dirty floor in what appeared to be a cozy bedroom like one from his youth, save for the bars on the window. A bare, army green cot, fastened to the ground, was the only furniture. His hands were zip-tied and thoughts of using anything as a weapon slowed with the realization that his captors had planned ahead. The room was spartan.

The undressed windows showed little light from the outside,

none of it natural, so Lopez figured some time had passed since some *hijo u hija'e puta* had knocked him out. At any rate, he really had to pee. While he felt no attachment to the room, he still had some standards.

There wasn't a bucket around and he didn't want to wet his pants. First, he used the cot to get himself to a kneeling position. Next was a shuffle on his knees to the door. The soreness in his legs was nothing compared to the pain in his head. He gave a slight rap to the outside before scooting back on his haunches.

Lopez shouldn't have been surprised at seeing *la soldado*, but her dark locks, caramel skin, and tight-muscled body would jolt any man. Suppressed recognition reflected in each others' gaze before he turned away and grunted. With his writhing legs, he didn't have to work to spell out the situation for her.

She approached him at once and helped him stand with a firm grasp on either side of his shoulders. He limped down a hallway as she led him from behind to a bathroom. Once there, her hands unzipped his fly, and his excitement allowed him to aim without any aid. He felt a gun barrel along his tingling spine to show she was still in charge.

Lopez cleared his throat when he was finished, and she pulled his pants outward so he could rearrange, restock, and restore his accouterments. His quick hip motions showed he wanted to waste no time getting himself squared away, but it was a delicate task given his arousal and inability to use his hands. Physiological response proved a nemesis to any sense of prudence.

La soldado cocked her gun. If the threat was meant to make him go limp, it didn't accomplish its aim. Her hands stayed on Lopez's waistband, only refastening his zipper when he calmed himself down and was enclosed. She puffed a breath on the nape of his neck when she returned her handgun to its holster, again taking his back and biceps to walk back to his room. Once there, a shove back to the ground crushed any fantasy.

Lopez rolled over as the soreness from his waist to his toes calmed. At the doorway, *la soldado* held a bottle of water. She took a drink before squatting near him, her quads holding her as she placed the nozzle to his lips. She tilted the base to let liquid nourish him.

He didn't know if she gave a shit about the Geneva Conventions, felt sorry for him, or wanted to establish trust before interrogation. It didn't much matter. His infatuation was growing into respect, with a hint of admiration. His common sense had stayed in the backseat of the bus to Fajardo.

When the bottle was nearly empty, she took it and then stood. They exchanged glances and he gave a nod before she turned around and left, locking the door from the outside. He was alone again, restless despite fatigue.

12

Bad Cop, Good Cop

The heavier than expected sound of a rock hitting sand made Carey Riley open her eyes. She saw a coconut had fallen about a foot from her face. Woken from her dream, the impact nearly lit her up like a shot from the Beretta .22 compact handgun she'd had in the Chicago suburbs. The problem was she now felt less control.

She sat up and looked at the surf, a thirst rising up in her throat as an arid aspiration. Lucidity was present enough to keep her from sprinting to the ocean and taking a drink. Her shoulder-length, crimson locks felt itchy from not being washed in a while, no doubt lacking its usual luster to reflect sunlight. Her scant clothing did nothing for her confidence.

A *policía municipal* approached, wearing a starched blue uniform too warm for the surrounding air. He asked her if she was okay in broken English, probably reacting to her alabaster skin. On any morning before being taken by thugs, she'd wave and respond in broken Spanish about how she was okay, thank him, and ask him the location of the nearest public restroom. After escaping captivity, getting shot at, and acting as a derelict

72

laying low, the morning was anything from normal.

Carey missed her boy and her husband, was thirsty, hungry, and tired. Nothing was familiar and she hadn't a mobile phone to call a friend. She wasn't in the mood for diplomacy and couldn't commit to reasoned commands in her head to feign victim-hood for a helping hand.

She stood and responded with a phrase that included *coño, bobo,* and *tu madre.* With that not enough to make a pleasant impression, Carey reached toward the officer in what he took as aggression. His reading of the situation wasn't completely off but was still presumptive. Neither one expected this to go easily.

The officer grabbed her wrist, with a nervous chuckle. Carey tried to throw him off balance by sweeping her sinewy leg to his kneecap. His strength and bulk were too powerful. The officer struck her firm abs and she doubled over before he took out handcuffs and lowered her to a prostrate position on the sand.

The ensuing pat down was not necessary, if unsurprising. Carey knew from her experience with John's sperm donor of a father, as a stripper in the suburbs, and as a Hooters waitress that insecure men made a point to get handsy without her consent. She reminded herself of *la policía*'s sense of inadequacy in an attempt to steel herself as he ran his hands along her sides, to her chiseled waist, to her hips, and the outside of her legs.

She felt a quick need to protest but didn't want to give him any satisfaction. To her surprise, he led her to a standing position with a degree of reserve. He delivered her Miranda rights in Spanish as he led her away from the beach toward a parked squad car with a driver from the *barrio.* The arresting officer put a heavy hand on her head to lower it for the car as the driver turned the ignition.

Carey wanted to spit in his face, shout about police brutality, and otherwise make noise. Her more rational mind kicked in and told her body to relax and continue as submissive. If she wanted to see her son and husband again, the best way to to do that was to placate a man with legal authority.

The cruiser ambled at a relaxed pace along the beach and the further into San Juan toward the Metropolitan Detention Center. The driver mentioned picking up a burger on the way the station. The arresting partner mumbled something about wanting to get rid of garbage before he lit a cigarette and dangled it from the open window.

Carey breathed shallow breaths to resist the stench of smoke and sweat in the back seat. She was too tired to distract herself from a sense of doom and boredom, with her only hope that Ron had made enough inroads with the locals to lend an eventual hand.

At the detention center's holding, she traded her sarong, her underwear, and her button-down for loose-fitting, government-provided garb. She considered the modest clothing and footwear a welcome development during processing and being put inside.

"From one jail to the other," Carey said softly to herself as Spanish rattled around her. She willed herself to blend in.

* * *

Supervisory Special Agent Matt Russo put out his cigarette on the particle-board coffee table at his hourly rental room at the Saturn Motel in Little Haiti and cracked open an O'Doul's.

He had taken the afternoon off from the Miami FBI office and wanted to get a few tendencies out of his system before returning home.

Clara hadn't let him live it down when he'd lost his cool the evening before and gave his daughter a whiskey-overpowered kiss for bedtime. His wife's dressing down was a good kick in the ass, and he figured he needed his own space to sort problems out. The stained carpet at the Saturn Motel should have made him wary, but the space, or lack thereof, gave him what he needed more than booze.

The carpet varied in color from a dark yellow to khaki. Baby blue seahorses dancing on the beige wallpaper exuded more cheese than Liam Neeson's cameo in the third season of *Miami Vice*. The clerk who rented the room was still in the 1980s, with a feathered mullet to boot. It was enough to reinforce an alcoholic's sense of self-worth.

The quiet, the kitsch, and a place to smoke made Russo smile, despite his mood. It tickled his funny bone that a motel for drug deals, hookers, and johns had free WiFi. He set aside his FBI duties to research background for his friend, Ron. When back on the clock tomorrow, he would send subordinates to stake out any low-level thugs he noticed around him.

Next to his O'Doul's, his government-issue Toshiba laptop gave faint clicks as his fingers ran over the keyboard. Earlier on FBI intranet, he had saved several articles that took a close look at the Shelling-Polk Corporation's man, Russell Thurgood. Although Thurgood was connected with federal government contracts, the cowboy hat-wearing putz had a reputation for covering up dirty deeds at the local level.

Russo looked at some left-leaning sources for a difference of opinion from his employers and figured out that Thurgood's reputation stank more than the air in the cramped motel room. An exposition in *The Nation* exposed Thurgood's defense of a contraceptive pill that made women infertile and a narcotic that was found more lethal than heroin but was more widely-available with a prescription.

Thurgood proved adept at running interference with the press and international human rights groups. Shelling-Polk donated largely to charity groups to help those affected in the US while selling the remaining stock of contraceptives at a cut-rate to South and East Asian markets. The narcotic was still a hit with opioid addicts in small and mid-sized US towns from the Midwest to Appalachia.

Agent Russo lit another cigarette as he thought about the drugstore cowboy dickhead's threats to Carey and Ron, pushing him to dig further. On a San Juan blog, where days ago he'd read hearsay about Ron's fiasco in the jungle, Russo used Google Translate to get some local perspective about Thurgood. It wasn't positive.

The blogger hyperlinked to various websites, some right-wing and some leftist, alternately praising and criticizing Thurgood for either keeping commerce and the spread of freedom private or being a tool of politicians and businesses to exploit locals. Russo flicked ash off the knuckle of his index finger before plugging the number Ron had given for a Nokia burner phone.

"Hey, *pendejo*," Ron said. "I thought you'd never call. Local cops and residents got hard-ons both for and against any US mainland pricks, depending on the payout. So I hope you might have something juicy to share. Carey can take care of herself, but I miss her and will strangle the sonofabitch who thought taking her was a decent idea."

"You probably weren't looking to take on big pharma," Russo said. "Uncle Sam is turning a blind eye to the Shelling-Polk Corporation with their man pushing chemical death for profit. Russell Thurgood doesn't have a lovely reputation. I'll look at San Juan FBI to see if I can find leads on a guy you can trust."

"Thurgood reminds me of Defense Department desk jockeys while I was basking in the sun in Iraq," Ron said. "I got a police contact I might be able to trust and figure I've got at least a few *campesinos* who would like to skewer the moneyed asshole. Hold on a sec."

Russo finished his cigarette as he listened to Ron warning John to keep away from a stove top. He felt a twinge of guilt for Zoe then and cleared his throat before taking a drink of O'Doul's. He reminded himself that sobriety wasn't as difficult as losing his family.

The sound of a phone chiming from Ron's end interrupted Russo's thoughts. He restated to Ron how he could help and how they'd get to the bottom of events before they played out. His friend responded that he had to answer a call from another burner. The two pals had to cut the conversation short.

"Well, *amigo*," Russo said. "Call me whenever at this number. Much better than calling the office number on collect."

"*Entiendes, mano.*"

After they disconnected, Agent Matt Russo clicked on his laptop for more info on Thurgood and Shelling-Polk. He was about to leave his room as his hour reservation closed when a few knocks hit his door. Through the eye hole, he saw a girl ten years older than his daughter waiting to enter.

He opened the door. She asked him if he was her date.

Instead of brushing off low-level lawbreakers not even worthy of a misdemeanor charge, he ushered her inside and swiped a $5 Coca-Cola from the mini bar. He gave her his sport coat and ushered her to sit on the bed as he waited by the door. Track-marks showed on her sleeveless arms.

When the john showed up outside the peephole, Russo opened the passage and slugged him in the mouth and then the temple to knock him out. He then took the girl by her tender bicep out a side door to the lot and his Ford Taurus. She blushed when he opened the door to his front seat for her.

The only verbal exchange was first name introductions during the drive to Community Services. Russo stayed with her through admission and gave staff a twenty dollar bill to add her personal effects.

He pondered over whether he'd done his best to help the girl get on a better path as he drove to his family's condo in Coconut Grove. He let out a sigh before he lugged heavy legs upstairs to their unit entrance.

Inside, Russo tiptoed to his daughter's room. He kissed her on the forehead as she slumbered in peace. He left, hiding any nerves rustling beneath his skin.

In the bedroom he had shared with his wife until yesterday, he changed into a T-shirt and shorts under darkness. He approached Clara in the living room, the TV radiating her face.

When a commercial interrupted her show, he calmly asked her to join him at the kitchen table. He started boiling water while she clicked off the TV and took a seat. He soon joined her with matching cups of decaf Lipton.

Clara listened as he apologized for his recent behavior and told her he needed to help his friend, Ron. Looking into her eyes, he promised that a life of danger was behind him, but he was still loyal. She was asked to trust him as she had before.

There was nothing more important to him than the safety of his daughter and the woman who'd chosen to be his wife.

"I need a partner, Matt," she said. "I can't do this on my own. One thing you know about is duty, which also extends to your family. Can I count on you?"

Matt Russo nodded and reached out his hand. She took it at her own pace.

After finishing their tea, she invited him back to their bedroom to sleep. They settled in with his chest to her back to ready for eight hours of rest. His breaths matched Clara's. The tentative sense of peace was hypnotic.

13

Guardian

Blood rushed to Ron's head as he brushed John's hands from the stove and answered the Motorola burner given him by the Russell Thurgood. On the other end were a bunch of obscenities and loud, assertive statements in strained Spanish.

From what Thurgood eventually revealed, the hoarse, excited voice over the phone's receiver was the ebony-skinned man who had collected the dead call girl. The common denominator local, the pork pie he'd seen with the crony, corporate, cowboy, was in pain.

The yelling didn't stop until a suppressed round from a handgun could be heard. The ensuing laughter was too maniacal for what Ron expected. The cocky, slippery, Texas-accented baritone would have put him on edge if he hadn't heard similar belligerent bravado before.

Ron steeled himself to make a quick plan, follow instinct, or blend the two approaches, per usual. He listened for now.

"Better continue pulling your weight, Ron," Thurgood's voice said. "We got your number and Carey's in a desperate spot. She's more valuable than some spic shooter. It would be a shame to read about her hittin' hard times 'cause of local gangs. These beaners can go off the rails."

Ron thought the drugstore cowboy sounded too threatening to be in charge. The tone reminded him of wannabe mob chuckleheads in the Chicago burbs, echoing Nicky Ferranti's chutzpah before a .308 round from an FBI sniper rifle silenced it. The politician-smooth swagger over the phone sounded desperate. The pitch was elevated, unhinged.

If Thurgood hurt Carey, announcing it wouldn't encourage Ron to toe the line. Her well-being was an asset if it could be proved. Ron needed to show strength rather than subordination.

Ron held the cards. Pissing him off would be a very bad move for any guy who was bluffing, even if such an idiot held the attention of big pharma's Shelling-Polk Corporation. A veteran protecting his family could screw up anyone's ledger. The ante needed raising.

"Put Carey on the phone, you..." Ron demanded, calling Thurgood a four-letter word that had become a favorite of his buddy, Russo. "If you hurt a hair on her head, you'll soon meet a deranged Army veteran used to dealing with assholes like you."

The ensuing pause was palpable.

"Carey's unavailable," Thurgood responded with a forced cockiness. "You oughta know you got a lot to lose. Your lady can get all the attention she needs."

"Why should I take your word?"

"You don't have to. But things can happen. You could be calling down a world of hurt, friend. You got a boy. Where would you and he be if an accident were to happen to the place you sleep? There's no reason to put your little bastard in harm's way."

Amateur, Ron thought. He allowed a few moments of silence to dwell on a tangible tension, stifling verbal reaction as he watched John do a round of push-ups after dinner. His son's absence from preschool was regrettable, but the kid showed he was adapting well. Ron returned a wink when his son opened an alphabet book before a self-directed routine of reading, washing, and bed. The two exchanged a smile.

Ron interrupted the silence with an abrupt laugh over the phone to Thurgood's ear. He could picture the corporate hack flinching despite an array of private goons and political connections. John's mimicking laughter from across the room was enough for Ron to calm any worries before he responded.

"Some people never get out of their early twenties, Texas," he said. "I spent my post-college years warring for Uncle Sam. When I got tired of that, I came home and worked until I had to kill a few mobsters for free. I'll protect what I love; what makes you think you're any different?"

Thurgood could be heard trying to slow down his breath on the other side of the phone.

"Veterans high on their own *peyote* are only dangerous to themselves," he said. "If you try to take me on, you're bound to lose a lot more than sanity."

"You wanna bet? You may have picked on the wrong *hijo'e puta*," Ron responded before disconnecting the call.

Ron then returned to the kitchen sink to clean his dishes as John finished bathing before bed. He soon joined his son in the boy's room to look at pictures from a Marvel comic book Ron had ordered online. It was a routine the two shared to ready for sleep.

Before Ron returned to the living room, he poured himself

two fingers of Jim Beam from a fifth bought before Carey got kidnapped. Images of her smile and the way she made John giggle flashed in his head as he sat on the couch.

He furrowed his brow, put off-ease at his inability to check in on her over the phone. He figured he'd get John to Margarita in the morning. Her caring for John would help him fulfill threats to Carey's big pharma abductor.

After he made sure his loaded Beretta was on a side table, Ron grabbed a Mickey Spillane novel and sat with his whiskey. The kitschy chaos of the story and soft sting of the brown liquid allowed him to nod off for a few hours.

* * *

In the unconscious world, Ron's senses flashed back to a housing project in Mosul in 2004. In his dream, it was just before dawn and the heat in the Iraqi air had yet to become too oppressive. He was readying himself with the other three members of his fireteam to check a brick and mud shack for insurgents.

The targeted home was registered to a woman and three children, but CIA spooks shared wind of "radicalized Sunnis on the premises, engaged in belligerent activities." Ron, in essence, just wanted to look out for his fellow Jawas, protect noncombatants, and get the job done. He was always prepared to embrace the suck.

Grains of sand pelted his face before the sun's rays brought scorching air loaded with carcinogens, not that it worried him more than impending death around every piece of trash on the roadway or sly smirk through a headscarf. Broader questions still lingered in his subconscious.

The sectarian power vacuum between Sunnis and Kurdish Iraqis gave sociopaths the opportunity to grasp for religious and/or political straws to justify gangland thuggery. Honest work mattered less than ass-kissing and convenient friendships to justify the use of force. Innocents were caught in the middle.

In a way, Ron felt like he was back in the US, except the grudges had lasted longer and the thugs were suicidal instead of just stupid. That and surroundings tended to hold more lethal consequence.

When he knocked loudly on the door, he was happy his automatic defensive duck wasn't required to dodge a bullet. The loud guttural, deep voice on the other side of the entry didn't instill confidence. A translator nearby gave the expected message, an Arabic version of multiple four-letter words. The translator related the message to the inside that this was an inspection from Coalition Forces. Ron would've chuckled at the absurdity of the situation if the consequences weren't so deadly.

The next sound, though more muted in his flashback, was staccato automatic fire from Soviet-era AK-47s, followed by the eruption of M16 rounds. With his hands holding one of the M16s, Ron shot a few bursts on instinct. When his Army brothers' point man kicked in the door, the team was met with a loud crash and the wailing of a four-year-old, brown-skinned child.

In his mind's eye, Ron saw a man and woman with gunshot wounds on the ground by crying children. He knelt by the four-year-old as a crash sounded in the background. At that moment, Ron awoke from his nightmare.

Ron opened his eyes to his tearful four-year-old stepson,

whose puffs of breath were more worried than sad. His Army combat training and fatherly instincts sprung him into action. He grabbed his son in front of the couch and his Beretta from the side table before hitting the ground.

He was back in his living room in Fajardo, Puerto Rico, having fallen asleep on defensive surveillance. John was still crying in his arms when Ron looked from his spot to the house's entrance, into the kitchen, and from there to the hallways leading to bedrooms.

Ron saw a frying pan on the floor and a burner on the stove turned on high. Relieved with the apparent lack of gunshots, he told his son to stay on the floor before he got up at a ginger pace, turned off the stove, peered outside their house through a thin gap between the door and the frame, and then rejoined his son. The palm of his hand on John's shoulder and a returned glance was enough to give them some ease.

After standing, Ron tucked the Beretta in the back of his waistband and gave his son a hand up. He then went to the kitchen, took the pan from the floor, and got eggs and other supplies from the fridge. Ten minutes later, he joined his son on the couch with breakfast. Noticing the hour hand on the clock nearing half past seven, he clicked the on the TV and used the remote to find a cartoon to put John at ease.

"What if" thoughts swirled in Ron's head as he spooned egg and cheese into his mouth. As various illustrated characters pulled weapons on so-called bad guys on the TV, his mind shifted to his dream. Blood drained from his face as he thought about the possibility of John getting shot or growing up with a parent dead or disabled from gunfire. As tough cartoons on TV reminded John to *"di no a las drogas,"* Ron reaffirmed his decision to drop his son with Margarita before dealing with psychopaths on a power trip.

After the father and son were done eating and the TV bad guys lost, John brought his dishes to the sink before Ron cleaned them. After a quick shower for both, they made their way to Margarita's yellow trailer.

Along the way, Ron kept his ears and eyes open to unwelcome attention while trying to play down any worry. It was as if he was hungover and needed to stay on task. In a way, he was in his element.

The barrage of quick, but friendly Spanish that greeted them was too excited for Ron to completely understand. The words *amigos, contenta,* and *comida y música* stood out. He put himself at ease when John hugged the beaming Margarita and returned a natural smile, which was a good omen.

Ron held out his right hand to shake, which was quickly swatted away. He couldn't help but laugh. Margarita put a hand on his shoulder, much like his late Aunt Peggy. The gesture overwhelmed him with a sense of immediate calm that even his experience with enemies foreign and domestic couldn't extinguish. The two exchanged a tentative hug.

With mediocre ability to speak the local language, Ron communicated the need for Margarita to watch John around the clock for a few days so he could take care of problems. He offered some money to help with expenses, realizing at once he was already pushing the limits of awkwardness.

Margarita refused with a playful swat of her hand, saying something that included the word *mierda.*

After smirking, he exchanged phone numbers for emergency contact. He warned that there was bound to be danger.

With John pulling at her arm, Margarita retreated to the kitchenette to grab some *galletas.* With the boy at her heels, he continued to her futon after saying *gracias* for the treat. Upon her return to the sink, she rummaged around underneath in safety-locked cabinets.

After telling Ron in a slow, measured tone to *mantente calmado,* Margarita put 20 gauge shells on the counter before pulling out a Remington Model 870 Pump Action Compact by its grip in her left hand. She made it clear none of her digits were in the trigger guard. She gave a toothy smile.

A cool shiver ran up the nape of Ron's neck as he noticed in his peripheral vision that his son was fully engaged with his cookie and a Spanish-language picture book. The motherly woman who stood six feet away in the other direction just continued her smile before returning the gun beneath the sink and shrugging her shoulders. One moment after closing the small distance between her and Ron, she offered the young father *una galleta.*

"*No gracias,*" Ron said.

Margarita joined John on the futon, flashed Ron a smile, and gave a wave. She tousled the boy's hair and read some words as the four-year-old followed along.

Ron chuckled, gave her a salute, and headed back into the world to deal with *pendejos* too powerful for anyone's good. Despite worries about his wife, the events of the trailer put him in a decent mood. The parallels with his Aunt Peggy, the woman who raised him, were too strong to ignore. John was safe.

There were jobs that needed doing, and Ron felt up to the task. First, he'd head to the library to collect his thoughts and dig up intel.

14

Desperados

La soldado poured scalding water into a pan with two level scoops of instant Bustelo. The several minute-wait was nothing compared to the tedium of the last day. Though her skills were more honed to threatening and ending life, she had been relegated to guarding the life of an FBI hostage in a dilapidated two-story house outside San Juan, near Santa Cruz. About a week ago, she had blown her chance to kill the agent and found she now was more or less okay with the result.

Luis was still pimping his local sources and powers from the US mainland to see if Agent Lopez under her watch had had any other contact with any G-men beside Rodriguo de Salinas. From her boss's tone, it seemed he was nervous about losing control. He was erratic and moody when they spoke over her burner phone.

La soldado didn't respect those calling the shots. There was no love lost with the *pendejo*, Luis, and the boss's nerves put her on edge. Assistant Special Agent-in-Charge de Salinas, Luis's Fed-for-hire, seemed to think Lopez's life was worth prolonging, which was enough for her to part ways with the *narco*.

At least Luis had arranged a Sig Sauer semi-automatic pistol for her through an intermediary. The sidearm was more precise than the MAC-10 from the previous job. Precision complimented her skill. Her attention focused when an Oldsmobile rolled up in front of the house.

When a caramel-skinned driver got out and pointed a handgun at the house, a fellow helping *la soldado* keep guard opened fire and hit the back passenger side window of the car. Glass exploded before a boom ricocheted off the walls of the house. In no time, all hell broke loose.

A gaggle of AR-15s from the Oldsmobile pierced the air with rounds as *la soldado* hit the ground. She rested her right elbow on the tile, using her dominant arm to put the sights of the Sig Sauer on one of many shooters reloading their magazines. After semi-automatic fire stopped for a spell, she released controlled rounds to silence several cerebellums from again showing any sense of reasoning. With the correct hardware, the hundred fifty odd feet separating her from her prey made her moves "child play."

La soldado grinned at explosions of blood, happy to be in her element. A Ford delivery truck soon stopped a ways behind the Oldsmobile. Several extras from a 1980s Arnold Schwarzenegger action movie followed her line of fire, shooting automatic rounds from AK-47s. Two boys on her side in the house soon lost their lives when better-than-expected shots reached their foreheads.

A minute after clipping two gunmen in the head and lying low of returned rifle fire until it slowed, *la soldado* decided to flee while she still could. As thugs outside rushed to the front of the house under cover of automatics, she fled to the rear room where Agent Lopez was held. Keeping him alive was worth more than Luis had estimated.

In the next minute, she entered the captive's room and was pleased to see him alert. Whoever was advancing on them wasn't dicking around. Lopez's face projected alluring confidence, despite their position.

La soldado cut the restraints on Lopez's hands but did not offer him a gun. On her hands and knees, with her sidearm in her back waistband, she scurried from the house like a rabid rat retreating from a cat. She still was not sure about whose whims she was ultimately serving.

She led Lopez toward a hidden back door. The sound of heavy footsteps from the front of the house made her halt despite her own volition. The brush of her captive's head against her behind made her angry even though she heard a soft-spoken *perdón* uttered with manufactured calm.

The escape met a hiccup within minutes when they were faced with a caramel-skinned man standing in their path, pointing with an AR-15. *La soldado* froze, but her quarry raised himself on his knees, with arms raised until he could get to a standing position.

Roberto Lopez probably knew the worth of his life as well, given the circumstances. She decided to follow his lead until she could re-assume some control of the situation. The weapons in her toolkit included more than proficiency with weapons and lean muscle. Even in a warzone, she figured her allure would give her an edge.

* * *

Agent Roberto Lopez held out his hands in supposed surrender. When fresh handcuffs were offered, he feigned cooperation until positioning his forearms, placed on either side of the barrel of his aggressor's semi-automatic. He then knocked the rifle off aim, evading a shot with snake-like reflexes. The intruder, thrown off balance, relaxed his grip on the rifle enough for the FBI agent to acquire it.

The AR-15 gave Lopez the shot of adrenaline to shoot in the knee the prick who'd just wielded it. A crack to the goon's temple followed. The rush told him to make his way out and he told *la soldado* to toss her handgun to the side. He held the immediate hardware he needed to keep control.

The company of the *mujer* who'd been tasked with guarding him was considered a welcome bonus. He was drunk with newfound independence to overcome any doubts. Despite his usually more prudent sense, he let *la soldado* escape with him. She led the way.

In quick time, he and the fit woman were outside. The two ran opposite the road until they came across Toyota on a side street. They ducked behind it to evade fire from the house, soon volleying return rounds from the recently acquired AR-15.

After cries of pain or two from his aggressors, Agent Lopez used the butt of the semi-automatic to break the driver side window.

He was pleased that a fellow thug had already exposed wires from the steering column from a prior heist. The lock to the door had also been previously jimmied. He didn't take the time to appreciate his luck as he crossed the wires, bypassing the ignition.

Lopez realized he had diverted his attention from the gal

enough for her to take off on her own. She had instead stuck around. She appeared complicit and put her slim, sinewy frame in the passenger side after he unlocked the opposite door.

Lopez smiled, depressed the clutch, and moved the stick to first gear. She returned a simper as they drove off.

On the highway bypassing San Juan, he had to stop for petrol. He shifted the car into neutral and killed the engine. He told himself he was still in charge as he kept *la soldado* in his sights. While filling his tank, he took in the dark hair caressing her caramel-toned neck. When done, he returned to the driver seat and connected the wires to start the car again.

When raising his eyes to put his view back on the road before shifting the car to first gear, Lopez ventured a glance at his passenger's toned, caramel legs. Before putting his concentration back on the road, his gaze was met in the rearview mirror with pursed lips that reflected a measure of mischief. A hue of blush flushed his otherwise hardened cheeks before a flash from his right hit his neck.

The hurt of betrayal was worse than the pressure to Lopez's larynx, even if he should have expected both. The woman who'd been watching him apparently hadn't dwelt on the same illusions of infatuation. With another blow to render him passive, if not dead, his eyes closed with the sensation of the *mujer* moving him and adjusting the driver seat of the Toyota. Despite his crushed libido, he dreamed well.

His time at Quantico had meant to prepare him for contingencies. Either his machismo or his lust led him to react without prudence. He'd been the captive, the captor, and now the compromised. Long suppressed instinct awaited to take took hold once again when he awoke. All in due time.

15

Whack Jobs

Ron Riley thought about his son, happy he'd made the decision to trust John's safety to Margarita. Pissing off Carey's kidnapper had felt good, but the intensity of repercussions was bound to explode. He trusted John was out of the crossfire, for now.

The air was cool for April in the tropics, which suited him. It helped him concentrate, to keep a more level head. With what he'd learned yesterday before and during another shift at El Rococo, he realized he needed to keep his distance for a few days.

Before tending bar, he had stopped at Fajardo's Public Library, Biblioteca Electrónica Ricardo S Belavalto, to check Russo's intel and whispers he'd overheard from the *campesinos*. Through a database very much like ProQuest, he found public records matching what Russo had found about Russell Thurgood. Reading between the lines, he saw a connection with the Shelling-Polk Corporation and local shit shows, glossed over by overtures to encourage pursuit of the almighty dollar.

At El Rococo, the *campesinos* hadn't held back about their

beef with US mainland power. The name Rodriguo de Salinas peppered the farmers' gossip about *la corrupción*. Ron had lubricated the banter with libations, happy that tending bar allowed him to multitask.

After having served the fourth round of Medalla Light, Ron offered the men a complimentary shot of *ron blanco*, which wasn't refused. Words became looser when he offered peanuts and beer refills. After filling other customers' drinks, Ron returned to the *campesinos* to overhear discontent at not seeing their favorite *mujer* at the local gun club where they practiced.

"Dónde está *Señora Carey? Ella es una buena mujer y una buena tiradora,*" one of them had said. Where has Ms. Carey been? She's a good woman and a hell of a shot.

Ron wondered the same thing, appreciating the compliment. He gave the guy an extra shot of aged rum with a smile. The *campesinos* ponied up a good tip after Ron had refreshed drinks. He offered to call them a taxi, but a sober one among them ordered fried food and flashed Ron a smile before taking care of his *amigos*.

In the present evening, just after dusk, Ron waited to meet his friendly *uniformado*, Carlos Velez, after their run-in the other day and some words between a burner and a payphone. After a day of new clues and revelations, Ron had to admit that the smirking face of his *amigo* was welcome outside of his seemingly quiet house.

The last and only time Carlos had been there was to meet Carey and John. A sense of serene joy had permeated that atmosphere. Now there was only worry about what needed to be done.

After unlocking the deadbolt, Ron ushered Carlos inside. He got Jim Beam from the cupboard to pour two fingers per person. The fifth was put on a side table as the two sat on the couch.

"Got into *la mierda* with some *malditos pendejos*," Ron said after toasting and taking a sip. "There's some innocents in the line of fire along with my wife. Underhanded powers are pushing profit and the only other guy I give any trust is a Fed on the mainland. Can I add you as a confidant?"

Carlos nodded with a sober look in the eye.

El *uniformado*, fresh from work, sipped his drink as Ron retold the story of the attack on him and an FBI agent abductor, Carey's abduction, and the overdosing call girl in his living room. Then there was the visit with an ebony-skinned goon and later the cowboy hat-wearing boss, threats all around, and the realization he was dealing with a US mainland big pharma flunky by the name of Russell Thurgood.

After refilling their drinks with another finger, Ron put a palm on his Beretta as he told of distrust of San Juan's FBI heads. The bourbon helped Ron decide he preferred potential carelessness to inertia. He still kept his son's whereabouts close to the chest.

"Looks like you real desperate, *mano*," Carlos said. "I gotta admit I liked that *mujercita* who died a meter from where we sit. *Sobredosis, mierda;* she was good for information. With this *pendejo* from Texas, I'll help you out more than *la policía municipal* can. As far as the FBI, I'm not sure what I can do."

Ron met the unexpected look of sympathy, which appeared genuine, with a wan grin before he set his empty glass next to the fifth on the side table. Carlos and he ducked when a blast of shattered glass from the living room front-facing window erupted. The two hit the ground, rolling away from flames toward the kitchen and the door as another Molotov cocktail came through the window frame.

Tongues of fire licked at the spilled whiskey as Ron tucked his Beretta in his back waistband and, on elbows and knees, led Carlos to the room where John was thankfully not inside. With the rapid incineration of the front of the small house, Ron held his breath and got up enough to bust a window to the outside. The butt of the Beretta proved useful to shatter the glass.

Ron didn't hear any whiz of bullets. Thankful for that, he clamored outside, ducking and rolling as best he could. He crawled away, figuring the light thud in the chaos behind him was Carlos following with a less graceful exit. At about 200 feet or so away from the inflamed house, he grabbed his Beretta and rolled so he could look for any tactical advantage.

Carlos had fallen behind and was approached by three goons. Ron sprang to his feet on instinct. He aimed the Beretta, exhaled, and shot one in the calf muscle before the thug could aim his weapon. Another one dove and scurried for cover as Ron aimed at the remaining thug's torso, hitting him in the groin.

"What a clustertruck," Ron muttered to himself, using a four-letter word that rhymed. He shot in the direction of the one fleeing, hoping to ward off counterattacks before he sprinted toward the inferno to check on Carlos

Thankful that his police friend had simply stumbled, Ron scanned the periphery. He searched the shot aggressors before taking their Glocks and smacking their heads to knock them out. When one of the other Molotov throwers appeared in the edge of his left eye, a few rounds from his Beretta appeared to be enough to scare him away.

A shot from the house then nicked Carlos's left shoulder

before Ron collapsed to a crouch. He returned fire toward their persistent pursuer, knocking the thug down. The two continued to flee, as fast as they were able with Ron's support. When the flaming house was distant enough, the two stopped.

El uniformado collapsed on the ground, swearing as his right hand covered the flesh wound on the opposing shoulder. Ron listened as his acquaintance handed him a set of keys, fished from a pants pocket between winces. The bleeding man gave Ron an address in Carolina and described a Honda parked three blocks from the burning house. He smiled as Ron phoned emergency services with the Motorolla burner.

"You saved my life, *mano*," Carlos said. "Go to my rental. You can stay there for tonight and maybe a few days more. I can't pay you back now, but I'm a man of my word. Get the hell out of here before *la policía* make an appearance."

Ron grinned and took off, looking for the Honda. His pal would get the best help from the authorities. It wasn't in anyone's best interest for him to hang around.

Low standards were a blessing when Ron reached the rusted Honda, but it started as fast as a Formula 500 racer with a decent stereo. Janis Joplin's immortal words over the car's radio about freedom and nothing left to lose echoed in Ron's head as he drove off. He appreciated having a local connection. With a little help from a friend, he'd get by.

* * *

Day old, jail-issued clothes hung from Carey's petite, muscular frame as she sat up on the top bunk in a women's holding cell in the Metropolitan Detention Center. Jail was not an entirely new experience, even if she hadn't spent much time on the inmate side before. Her actions from the past day gave her a degree of acclimation.

Her first contact after admission had been friendly enough. The woman was an ebony-skinned, fit woman aged around 25 who addressed her with a Creole-accented English. They had met early the previous evening in a lesser populated area of the recreation area.

Carey usually warded off unexpected attention with a firm, if non-threatening, face. At the time though, it proved more important to be tactful when handling a jailhouse crush. She displayed a supposedly suppressed Sapphic interest to gain an ally. She took the woman's hand from the small of her back, giving it a squeeze.

Carey replied in her best Spanish that she could use a friend more than a lover. She told the ebony-skinned gal she was a cutie, but to keep her distance as Carey wasn't planning to stay long. A guard alarm kept them both from having to justify words with action.

Recreation was over. Carey had been saved by the bell only to be delivered to less welcoming quarters. She expected hostility from those sharing her cell and awaited a test of her mettle. She didn't rest well before the current morning.

When her cell was delivered in the morning what could be charitably described as sustenance, she dropped from her bunk, ready to defend herself. A brown-skinned, Amazonian-sized woman woke up and knocked her tray to the floor. The shiv in one the woman's beefy hands was as charming as the grunts given instead of words

Threats were a phenomenon with which Carey felt more accustomed than lesbian interest. In a way, she was thankful for a release that had nothing to do with sex.

Carey faked a right jab before slugging her aggressor with a left hook to knock her to the ground. She put her hand to the Amazonian's throat to check the pulse and give resuscitation or retaliation, as needed. With no need to play nurse, she retrieved a piece of the so-called food and swallowed it down in a few gulps.

The cell across the way looked on as she instilled the fact that she was no one's *puta*. She only needed to glare at any fellow cellmates to make them back off. Later in the community room, other prisoners showed her a chair as they watched the news.

The TV screen showed the man who'd kidnapped Carey. He appeared nervous, sweating despite being surrounded by air conditioning. The Shelling-Polk Corporation executive, Russell Thurgood, as identified by the screen, was happy about prospects west of San Juan. The slimy *gringo* recently received the blessing of Secretary of Economic Development Juan Ramón Sanchez-Riera.

No one else in the fairly small transient, criminalized community seemed to have been paying attention. Thoughts of messing with the power structure swirled in Carey's head as she returned to her cell. She put her head to rest on her bunk and waited for time to pass.

Getting kidnapped, going to jail, and proving she was no one's bitch was never in the cards when Carey moved to Puerto Rico with her husband and son. Worries shifted to Ron and John, but she had to stay in the moment. Life had grown interesting in her short time behind bars.

"Within twenty-four hours, these bastards have to either charge me or release me," Carey muttered to herself, hoping the cops inside would have better tasks to do than to add to the inmate count.

Images of the beach in front of her house filled her thoughts. The crash of the tides and the smiles of her men lulled her into unconsciousness. With pleasant dreams so far away from reality, she didn't rest with ease.

16

Bitter Sweet

The green of palms whizzed by the 1999 Subaru Impreza as it drove westward on the PR-2 Highway toward Bayamón. Wind whirred by the stolen car, audible but unable to sound out the snores of the unconscious captive laying in the backseat. *La soldado*, having bunched her locks into a small ponytail, sweated through her nerves as she thought through her options. She longed for a joint, a drink, a kill.

The sweat on her neck drew trails across skin that was becoming too grimy for comfort. She'd stolen the Subaru, grabbed what food she could, hydrated, and kept to less-traveled roads. She'd been watching her valuable cargo for almost a day, knocking him back out at least once during their travels. A necessary part of the battle was dirt and the rush of adrenaline, but fatigue was setting in.

The ride allowed her time to consider her options with the criminal triumvirate of Luis, *gringo* big pharma, and FBI Assistant Special Agent-in-Charge Rodriguo de Salinas. New front lines were forming.

The attack they'd fled from outside Santa Cruz involved too

many expensive guns to belong to low-level junkies, even if that's what was reported over radio news to be the cause. She wasn't sure Luis had the balls or much reason to carry out the attack but did not put it past him to go against de Salinas's calls for tact.

The gunfire, even if it resulted in mostly *Boricua* casualties, wouldn't play well with the Shelling-Polk Corporation's Russell Thurgood. As for the *gringo* cowboy, radio news recently reported that he got the okay from Secretary Sanchez-Riera. The slippery Fed and he wanted to appear legit, and Luis didn't attract the right kind of credibility.

Luis's ineptitude prompted a sense of *libertad*. She already thought her boss was *un mama bicho*, a kiss-ass weakling, so dissolving that alliance was easy. *La soldado* gauged her captive's worth from the threats on his life and his plucky response to those threats. Preserving his and her life became her main focus for now. She needed an ally or two.

La soldado took a ramp off the Expreso Jose de Diego just before Bayamón to meet with a man who would be straight with her, if not on the level with anyone else. The guy and she were acquaintances from ten years of age, lovers on and off at fourteen, and since then, business partners trading weed. She knew the *cabrón*, Oscar, was trustworthy enough due to his hate for authority.

A series of turns led to a gravel road. *La soldado* pulled to a pathway that led to what could only be described as a shack held together by asbestos and lime-green vinyl siding. The front had a few broken-out windows, a sign of trouble despite the ways of her would-be host. She immediately put the Subaru in reverse and had to stop when she heard the unmistakable eruption of a shotgun.

Pellets struck the hood of the car, rendering the engine useless as she realized more entrenched interests had already encroached on her plan. Any guns playing to her strengths were underneath the front passenger seat, hidden from the casual attention of any authorities, and more readily available to her captive. Shouts from the shack implied she'd have to play passive until she could find an advantage.

La soldado hoped improvisation could be as useful as access to quality firepower. She tried to appear non-threatening while exiting the Subaru with ears and mind open, palms open to the sky.

"Marisol," Oscar shouted after exiting the shack. He continued with measured steps, calling for her to keep calm and cooperate for both their sake. *La soldado*, Marisol, heard him and maintained her poise with the theory her hostage might be more worthwhile than originally suspected. She wanted to do right by her weed-dealing pal, but the shotgun blast had been enough to even put the coolest customer on edge.

Oscar approached opposite her, put a hand on her right shoulder, and flicked his eyes to the handgun lower at his waist, knowing full well that she was a lefty. Marisol tried to appear calm as she took a knee before him and placed her dominant hand just beneath his pistol. She winked before giving an authentic-enough punch to her pal's gut and taking the gun with swift hands.

Marisol rolled on the ground and shot to avoid chaos and fight back. Lights in the sky and the flare of adrenaline to her nerves proved negotiation to be overrated. Oscar proved to be her ally until his life took a critical blow.

* * *

Agent Roberto Lopez's eyes opened after the bangs of a shot-gun and a semi-automatic rifle. His body and subconscious had prepared him for a fight. On the floor in the backseat of Subaru, he found a weapon.

With AR-15 in hand, he switched off the safety, rolled outside, and aimed as a green-shaded cottage erupted in explosions of gunfire. He began shooting under the assumption the chamber was empty, with his aim proving the greatest advantage.

The shooting thugs he put in his sights dropped faster than stones in the Caribbean as he focused his rage, fueled by a crushed libido. FBI firearms training helped as he maneuvered and picked off a few goons with measured breaths. When eruptions stopped, he took a look around, looking for weak points, rogue assailants, and other targets.

On the ground, between the Subaru he'd escaped and the ramshackle *cabaña* before him, Roberto Lopez saw *la soldado*, his seductive jailer, matching his aim toward now dead goons. Next to her was a guy whose belly was eviscerated with shots. With any apparent threat neutralized, Lopez reverted to his Quantico training to find out more from the living. He closed the distance with the *mujer* at once.

After slapping the pistol from *la soldado's* left hand, he put pressure on the wounds of the man prostrate to the ground. They didn't have to worry about witnesses, anyone nearby had either died or dispersed. The air seemed calm; too much so. *La soldado* pulled Lopez away to engage with the wounded.

"Marisol…Marisol," the man uttered as tears joined rivers of sweat over caramel skin. Words sensible only to the two of them led her to embrace him with her athletic breasts on his chin. With a nod back and forth, *la soldado* used her hands to snap his head at an angle, breaking his trachea. The engaged muscles from her trapezius to her forearms didn't have a chance to relax before they were wracked with subdued cries.

Lopez grabbed *la soldado* by her muscular waist and wrestled her to the ground after laying the AR-15 at a non-threatening, yet accessible distance. He protected any expected shots to his groin, which left the head above his shoulders more open to attack. She clipped him under the nose enough to draw visions of transient flashing stars before his eyes.

When his vision returned, she was in a place of power on top, with her legs on either side of his rib cage. Thankfully, she hadn't grabbed his rifle. He noticed the bleeding wound gracing the outside of her right thigh, the pain from which his free arms and fingers exploited before his breaths could become incapacitated with her slight weight and the strength of her hips and hamstrings. He took advantage of the pain from the flesh wound and rolled out from underneath her.

Realizing he'd grown excited beneath his waist, Lopez felt hints of self-consciousness when he used his greater weight to pin *la soldado* to the ground. After grabbing her wrists and holding them to her side, he tried to appeal to the emotion he'd seen her exchange with the dead man with the belly wounds. He didn't want to be more aggressive than he had to be.

Lopez realized then he was too preoccupied with lascivious lingerings to be a proper FBI agent. Conflicted urges about his captive put him in an ethical quandary. He had to show even greater restraint than that from his pants to establish a hint of trust.

Putting his mouth to her ear, Lopez spoke directly to *la soldado*.

"*Quiero ayudarte.*" I want to help you. He wasn't sure why, but baser instincts were a good hint.

She bit her lower lip and pushed off the ground against him. Her light brown eyes pierced his before she grimaced and nodded toward the shack. It was obvious she needed control as well.

"Vamos en la cabaña," responded *la soldado* named Marisol. Let's go inside.

Lopez more than wanted to lose himself. Instead of giving in, he retook his rifle before helping her up. He led her to the shack for first aid, where they found a soiled if functional, water closet.

Resting against the door frame to the room, he snuck glances as she peeled off her fatigue pants and her boots. She did this as she leaned on her behind against a stained white sink that looked dirtier than her simple boxers.

He knew he was close to crossing a line. He didn't much care; they weren't trying to kill one another. There were more pressing matters, like working together to stay alive.

With the semi-automatic in one hand, Lopez used the other to help clean her wound with iodine they'd found in an off-kilter medicine cabinet. He determined a lower caliber rifle round had nicked her thigh, missing the femoral artery with ease. She handed him a bandage and gauze, wincing to the degree that normal people did with a paper cut. With his free hand helping hers, they gave her upper right leg a tight wrap.

When he finished playing medic, he relieved himself in the toilet, his rifle in one hand, appendage in the other. Just outside the door frame, she tested her leg for balance as he finished. After finding a slight limp to help distribute the weight, she led him to a makeshift kitchen and looked under a grubby-looking sink. She found a nearly full fifth of *ron blanco* and took a swig.

The heat and humidity in the air lingered as they took care of each other without exchanging a word. They exchanged furtive glances, unsure of what to do. There was a degree of illusive trust, but he still wasn't entirely sure whether to screw her or kill her. Survival was almost as exciting to him as sex at this point.

It's likely she was also indecisive, even when she kissed him. Their tongues flicked between lips before Lopez pulled away. He took a swig of the rum. Somehow, instinct made him peck her cheek before getting to necessities; no time in the moment for romance.

Lopez found a half-full box of cornflakes in a cabinet, taking a handful now and saving the rest for the road. Marisol returned to the WC to relieve herself and put her pants and boots back on. With the rum bottle in her left hand and the AR-15 in his right, they made their way back outside, cradling cornflakes and other contraband with care.

They navigated on foot to get away from the scene of their recent gun fight. Ahead of the duo, a late 1990s Toyota Tacoma, with a cover over the bed, was pulled off near a ditch a few miles from the road leading out of town. The owner was peeing further away in a field as they crept up to the vehicle.

While the victim was otherwise engaged, the two opened the unlocked doors, happy the good man had made the mistake of leaving his keys in the ignition. *La soldado,* Marisol, buckled her safety belt after her company had done the same and turned the key. The rumble of the engine put the pisser on alert, but he was too late, holding on to his pants and cursing as the truck peeled off.

On the way due southeast, Lopez tried his best to stay out of traffic, willing his attention off the mysterious, lethal beauty riding shotgun. She took another pull of rum before offering him more. He declined, simply driving and trying to act normal in some way.

He knew they needed time to unwind. He was not even sure why he was staying with the woman who'd shot at him, abducted him, and kissed him, most recently. Justifications wavered between lust and his state of limbo with any future in the FBI. Questions swarmed his conscience as his tired eyes tracked the road.

As daylight dimmed into dusk, Lopez headed south of Caguas into the mountains of Cordillera Central. With the change in gradient, greenery, and the expanse of space, he decided to stop off the PR-52 Highway in an unpopulated area near the Rio Turabo to collect his thoughts.

He and his captive, or captor depending on the perspective, had to figure out where they were headed, and whether to strike back at or stay anonymous to forces larger than themselves. The peace of the mountains and palms was welcome.

Marisol, apparently of the same mindset, seemed pleased to play along. The first thing they needed was a dip in the river to rinse off the stink of sweat, blood, and dust that had accumulated.

They undressed, with him looking the other direction as the soothing, cooler water ran over sore limbs. When he snuck a glance back toward her, he saw her protecting her right leg, cleaning her top and pants in the water while rubbing water over her arms, abs, and left leg.

The cool water wasn't enough to keep Lopez limp when he emerged from the river. In the truck bed, he found clean-enough blankets, one of which he wrapped around himself.

He hung the other on the passenger side door. She limped to the Tacoma shortly thereafter, replacing the blanket with her rinsed clothes.

Lopez built a fire, using the truck's cigarette lighter and assorted kindling and fuel he'd found. He sat next to her as they munched on cornflakes and shared the rest of the rum to get numb. The smoke-tinged air grew cool.

Marisol flashed a grin before opening her blanket and asking if he'd like to share her body heat. He had no choice but to smile and oblige. After light exercise, her sinewy left leg wrapped around his abs, he carried her into the covered truck bed to catch some rest. He kissed her neck before unconsciousness gripped them both.

Before the sun showed again in the sky, Marisol surprised him with a new twist when he awoke on a blanket crushing tall blades of grass. Where was the girl? And just as important, where was the truck?

17

The Scheme

Ron stayed away from anywhere familiar, which meant no visits to John, nor to his work at El Rococo. The silence of Carlos's rental for the past day was enough to push Ron to clean the smallish space. Fumes from the cleaning liquid and tight muscles from repetitive swishing and wiping forced him outside for fresh air.

Soon back inside, he occupied himself with inspecting and cleaning his Beretta, nuking what he could find in the fridge, and checking his burner phones every fifteen minutes or so. With the ring of the landline, Ron found himself wanting to answer with the eagerness of a puppy waiting for a piece of raw liver. He let it ring until the answering machine announced he'd missed a collect call.

Curiosity made him wait by the phone until it rang again. When it did, he snatched the phone before the first annoying melody could finish.

On the receiver, automated Spanish revealed a collect call from a local pay phone to make him grin. Ron accepted the charges. He was interested in any news and Carlos was ultimately picking up the bill. Without uttering his own breath, Carlos gave him an interrogative hello.

"*Qué pasa*, Carlos?" Ron replied. What's up?

Carlos updated Ron that his wound was easily treated by emergency doctors and he'd been released in enough time to grab eight hours sleep at a San Juan hotel. Carlos added that Ron was welcome to pay for just enough drinks to not send him to the hospital again with alcohol poisoning.

First, they had to quickly move. He explained in forced "American" that was understandable only to Ron.

A pal at the Metropolitan Detention Center had just told Carlos about a feisty *gringa* who could be Carey. Pretty, pale-skinned redheads behind bars in Puerto Rico were as rare as trustworthy politicians. Carlos said he'd send some patrol officers to set up a meeting with the inmate and negotiate a release if she could answer some questions which few people but Carey could answer.

Ron was thankful and gave some questions and answers, pausing for his friend to transcribe. With the hope that his wife was safe and the knowledge his son was in the caring hands of Margarita, he told Carlos that he needed to be on the move from his friend's apartment. He didn't wait for a response before asking *el uniformado* if he was cordial with any of the *campesino* customers at El Rococo.

"Can't say I'm too tight with any of them, but I roll with a few," Carlos said, attempting accents he had heard in bootleg copies of movies. "They's good boyos. *Amigos*, ya might say."

"You Ice Cube, Tommy Chong, or Joe Pesci?" Ron muttered before giving a chuckle. "I wanna get in touch with a fella with skin in the game and hardware to boot. I comped a few drinks at the bar while staying wise to chitchat, but as you probably know, I can't go around there no more."

"I dig," Carlos replied after a hint of hesitation. He continued, trying to mimic another movie set in the inner city US. "Just tell it to me straight, yo."

Ron rolled his eyes and explained that he had heard the fellas railing against the Shelling-Polk Corporation and an FBI Agent named Rodriguo de Salinas. He needed like-minded associates to teach a lesson to the dickhead, Russell Thurgood, and his collaborators.

"You need an army, *mano?*" Carlos asked.

Ron said he'd appreciate whatever local help he could get. He kept to himself the *campesinos'* possible connection to Carey. The absence of the favorite *mujer* from the gun club might prove another useful card to play to win allies.

Carlos responded about a real *cabrón* named Willy. The *campesino* in question headed a hydroponic farm for all types of products, legal and not so much. He held a lot of sway. The guy had *cojones* and firepower, to boot.

"*El es intelligente, un hijo'e puta,*" Carlos said. He's intelligent and quite a dick.

"*Maravilloso.*"

Ron continued that he needed to set up a meeting away from El Rococo, but not too far from Carolina and San Juan. He wanted to rally troops to help with a cause and fight now that Carey and John were more or less safe. Meeting in a spot that wasn't habitual to him was best to throw off any trails and allow any potential soldiers to bow out if they didn't feel like "kicking some ass."

Carlos responded that he'd shortly set plans up, noting that he had some cards to play due to looking past Willy's less legal business. He added that Ron's payment now included the promise he'd help *el uniformado* find a loose lady, *una mujerzuela,* when his *gringo* friend was safe with his wife and son.

"*Lo conseguiste tio,*" Ron responded. You got it, man.

He affirmed that payment wouldn't be a problem if they all lived to survive the fall out from pissing off politically and *narco*-connected businessmen. Love-making and rum were how all action heroes celebrated when the gunfire calmed, right? A comradely chuckle greeted him on the other end of the phone before they both disconnected.

* * *

Agent Matt Russo lit a Marlboro and sipped decaf espresso on the patio at the City Center Starbucks in Miami Beach. The early evening's fading rays of sun over the city were beautiful shades of orange and peach, which spring break tourists shared for "friends" on Flickr and Facebook to covet.

Russo didn't have time for cordial social networking or taking in the sights. He was too busy after work hours helping his buddy Ron. The intrigue was far more stimulating than any wannabe's soy caramel Macchiato.

At the office, he had copied several items from the FBI intranet to his Toshiba laptop. He now used an encrypted browser to grant himself a bit of added security from prying eyes. The cigarette had burned to a butt, scorching the knuckles in Russo's right hand when a CNN RSS feed showed the latest on Russell Thurgood.

The Shelling-Polk Corporation drugstore cowboy had gone from making friends in San Juan to having "alleged ties" to Puerto Rican illicit drug distributors following a number of shootouts reported on local blogs and Twitter. Although allegations didn't link Thurgood officially, Russo's intuition led him to suspect those in charge.

Local chatter from progressive sites also cast shade on San Juan's FBI man, Assistant Special Agent-in-Charge Rodriguo de Salinas. Saved intranet memos added to Russo's suspicions. Higher-ups in the federal government were not above lawful justice. His old boss in Chicago, sitting in the federal pen, again came to mind.

Caffeine and nicotine rushed to Russo's brain as he delved deeper. A stream of banter coming out of the San Juan branch the last day or two talked about an agent having potentially gone rogue. From the day Ron reported the automatic weapons fire exchange in the jungle along a highway to San Juan, followed by Carey's kidnapping, an Agent Roberto Lopez had gone underground.

Further digging led Russo to determine Agent Lopez had followed orders from his superior, Assistant Special Agent-Charge de Salinas, to take a potential witness, read Ron, into San Juan from Fajardo. It was then that official communication with Lopez had ceased. He noted a lack of official chatter over Lopez until recent gunfire outside San Juan and Bayamón.

Russo swore under his breath when he read that Lopez was considered compromised, armed, and dangerous. Just then, his burner buzzed. He didn't recognize the number and gave an alias to protect his peaceful life in Florida.

"Johnson's Plumbing, we'll clean your pipes," Russo said. "Just tell us which tube you want to unclog."

"Erectile Dysfunction Anonymous called from their home office in Wichita, Kansas," Ron's voice said over the receiver. "They said you'd given them my number if they needed to collect on a debt? You need help, man? I told them it's natural for guys your age. I can get back to them if you want and keep them updated of your financial situation."

After a four-letter word, Russo asked what the "wanna-be Jarhead" wanted. It was more like camp than the war zone, with the verbal shrapnel a good antidote to new found domesticity and life as an underutilized FBI desk jockey.

"You're too far away for a kick in the ass," Russo said. "Do you want a hand or are you gonna keep busting my balls?"

"What else are my tax dollars paying for?" Ron asked before pulling it in a little bit. "Alright. I know you're being a friend more than a Fed. Sorry. We've both saved each others' asses. Now, what can you do for me?"

"Dick," Russo said before continuing.

He filled in his friend on the intel he'd uncovered about Russell Thurgood and his "alleged" allegiances with more local, if less well-reputed, drug dealers. The Puerto Rican FBI office was likely compromised through bureaucracy, ineptitude, or treason, starting with Agent Rodriguo de Salinas. Russo added he wasn't inclined to call in the troops. He could still point Ron in the direction of potential if unconventional, help.

"San Juan-based FBI Agent Roberto Lopez went off the reservation after your adventure with the Dodge and the shooter in the jungle. Higher-ups have written him off as rogue, but you might have a pal if you happen to cross paths. You mentioned a Latino who was a good shot as part of the reason you got away. Serendipity, maybe?"

"What are we involved in now?" Ron said. "Hollywood movies don't rely on this level of coincidence. You have any clue on how to get in touch? If he's the same guy, he helped me escape automatic gunfire only armed with a Springfield

1911. The dude could be useful."

"There might be a trail being carved out," Russo said before explaining further.

Using Google Translate to understand several articles on *Periódica El Expresso De Puerto Rico*, Russo had done some armchair reconnaissance. He read about a shootout outside of Bayamón that raised several red flags.

Shots from a semi-automatic aimed from a broken down Subaru killed at least two men near a shack, with another guy dead outside with a shotgun blast to the gut and a broken neck. *Policía municipal* responding to the scene commented about the precision from the semi-automatic shots. It looked professional.

Another article, which was more of an entertainment piece, was about a guy whose Toyota Tacoma was robbed while he was taking a piss off of a ramp near the shootout. The hijacker headed east on the expressway. It was like in a Steven Seagal movie, the newspaper reported with sensationalized pluck.

Random public police chatter from an APB on the mess outside of Bayamón related signs of a late 1990s Tacoma heading southeast. From the few officers on traffic control, a Tacoma was last seen near Caguas. It was there, in the present, that the trail went cold.

"It's a stretch, but something could pan out," Russo said. "Having another local ally couldn't hurt."

"Dealing with coked-up mobsters running a strip club was somehow easier," Ron remarked, referencing his and Russo's first adventure in the Chicago suburbs.

He continued that he appreciated Russo's input and would try to catch the latest on local media. Ron said Carey and John seemed to be in good hands, so he was in the business of looking for friends to help throw matches on the gasoline spill dumped in his part of the world.

"I'll keep my burner on, available to check in when not at work," Russo replied. "You'll see your wife and son again soon."

"*Nos vemos, mano,*" Ron said. "*Gracias.*"

The two signed off as pal do.

Russo shut down his Toshiba laptop and bussed his table before heading home in the Ford Taurus to Clara and Zoe. Heat flushed to the nape of his neck, tingling his ears as he pulled into the condo parking lot. The need for booze was tugging at his nerves, but his breathing and pulse calmed when he went inside.

His palms stopped sweating when he pecked his daughter on the forehead as she rested, oblivious to the dangers of the world. Across the hall, he shed his clothes before joining Clara, who was resting in bed with Jodi Picoult's latest bestseller. Within a half hour, the desk lamp serving as her reading lamp was out. His pulse slowed along with hers as they found slumber in each other's arms.

18

A Fuego

With early morning spring air warming Carey's face over slop at the start of her third day in jail, she ate with a few more allies along with the ebony-skinned gal from the introduction to her stay behind bars. She was learning to fit in until US law mandated her to either be charged or released.

Carey smiled at her new acquaintances before going to dump the remainder of her "food" in a bin collected for compost. Although the experiences her fellow inmates told tarnished her latent belief in the so-called justice system, she had to remain optimistic about getting out. Visions of her son teased her head as she walked from the communal mess hall to the fenced-in recreation area.

In the fresher air, Carey passed a baggie of brown tar heroin from her ebony-skinned gal pal to whom she had discovered was a middlewoman between inmates, police, and the Martinez Familia Sangeros mob. Her gal pal had informed her outside the showers yesterday to comply unless she wanted a beehive full of enemies.

The middlewoman pushed Carey's ebony-skinned friend

into a fence after getting the baggie. Carey was the only one to make a stand as guards acted oblivious. Despite the eruption of fists and epithets, no one paid any attention until the bully was yelling in pain.

Before guards intervened, heat, pride, and a flush of blood ran through Carey's spine to her head. She punched the bully in the nether regions, swiping a leg to drop the bitch as a guard blew a whistle. Authority intervened before lasting harm could befall anyone.

"Deberías cooperar, puta," muttered a voice that was somehow a mix of crunching gravel and the shriek of a cat. You should cooperate.

A guard frisked Carey, pushing her to the ground until his superior yelled for calm. An official-sounding, male voice sounded above any surrounding murmurs. Her ebony-skinned acquaintance and the bully faded to the background.

Carey hadn't seen the guard before. He had tree trunks for arms and escorted a trim-looking functionary toward her. The smaller man stood out, dressed in a short-sleeved white button-down and a plaid necktie that contrasted with his Ray-Bans.

With a wave of necktie's hand, the muscle gave Carey's right bicep muscle a firm, but not-quite-aggressive grasp before the two led her back toward the mess hall and eventually to the offices where she'd been processed. It was nearing the seventy-two-hour mark for charge or release.

From the Spanish spoken to her, Carey translated that she was being told to relax and that someone from the outside had been asking about her. She was told to write down some responses to poorly-transcribed questions.

Concerns about her drugstore cowboy captor overtook

immediate worries about surviving jail. She willed herself to play along and gave answers only her and Ron knew: Aunt Peggy, Dinty Moore, California Clipper

She wondered if Thurgood had taken Ron. Were her boys safe? What did the pricks need her for then? Did they just get a kick out of manhandling women? As the necktie-donning functionary and another muscled goon led her to a squad car, Carey attempted acquiescence.

She slowed her breath to calm her heartbeat when her head was lowered so she could take a place in the backseat. The lack of handcuffs, a blindfold, or any other restraints could be read as positive, but a sense of skepticism persisted. Paranoia told her that thugs were looking to find her easier to "deal with." Precautions weren't needed if her destination would soon be death.

Carey stayed calm as the muscle drove, with necktie riding shotgun. She recognized the route toward Carolina and willed her breaths to increase. When traffic grew barely existent, she saw an opportunity.

The men started to panic when she showed signs of hyper-ventilating. She didn't have to work hard to provoke a sense of unease. Her chest rose and fell in a way that wasn't quite sexy.

The muscle pulled the squad car to the side of the road on the side of the river east of Trujillo Alto, put the car in neutral, applied the parking brake, exited, and then opened the rear driver side door to pull her out. He ripped open her shirt to start administering CPR, per American Red cross training.

Necktie soon stepped near, stayed standing, and flipped open a mobile phone. He spoke with surprising calm, waving a stray passerby to continue on as his associate acted.

The muscle hooked up a portable AED to her right breast and her left abdomen, remembering first to turn the device on. The muscle moved the index and middle finger of his right hand to her carotid artery to check for her pulse. Its rate was heightened, even more than his when her jaw made a split-second turn to sink her incisors into his life-affirming digits.

Carey followed her bite with a blow to the muscle's temple. After jumping to her feet and tearing off the AED pads, she rushed to knee necktie in the gonads and collect his mobile, closing it as excited Spanish sounded from the receiver. The pavement, still wet with an early morning downpour, propped the functionary's head after he collapsed to the ground. A punch to the temple knocked him out.

It took some finagling to get necktie's white button-down shirt off, and though it was dirtied from the ground and a bit big, Carey preferred it to the exposure of her breasts under a torn shirt. She pocketed the flip phone and removed the Glock semi-automatic from the muscle's holster. The squad car ran in neutral, keys still in the ignition as she removed $80 total from her captors' wallets. Her return to freedom had gone smoother than expected.

In the squad car, happy with her ability to drive stick shift, Carey headed west toward the PR 199. On the highway, she turned on the siren and drove well over any posted speed limit, keeping her eyes peeled for lawbreakers to steal from. A Mustang speeding out from a Shell gas station gave her motive, ability, and desire to change costume. She figured the opulence of the car and its unblemished exterior made it a rental.

When the Mustang pulled over, Carey parked her first getaway vehicle much closer than police regulation mandated, nearly nudging the rear bumper. She knew her appearance wasn't in line with the official police, so short distances and timing were of the essence. She whipped open her door and closed the distance to her mark's driver side.

Sudden recollections of being chased by the mob in Chicago's western suburb of Woolrich hit her as she reminded herself to be as polite as possible and not threaten with her newly-acquired sidearm. The Mustang's window rolled down.

"No hablo español," said the middle age driver, whose skin was nearly as pale as her own. A woman with the same age and complexion sat in the passenger seat. *"Lo siento."*

Carey needed the car. The daylight hours, the initial appearance of authority, and behavior of the driver reminded her she didn't need to be a bitch about it.

"You were well over the speed limit, *señor,*" she said with a slight Puerto Rican accent. "I'll need you and the *señora* to step out of the car and let me see your passports."

When the couple complied. Carey dropped the cruiser's keys and the passports to the ground, taking the next second to get behind the wheel of the Mustang. She turned the ignition, stepped on the gas and left the tourists with the squad car. She figured they'd report the Mustang, cash in on any travel insurance, and have a good story for friends.

Carey turned south on the PR-52 Highway, dialing for Ron's Nokia burner on her new phone. When the voicemail greeting responded, she left a message that she was free and well. They'd always wanted to check out the countryside south on the island, so her words left the hint of where she was headed.

She was just north of Caguas when she pitched necktie's phone out the window. Ron would discover a way to stay above the heat from police authority and the kidnapping pharma-connected cowboy. He would protect their son while doing his best to find her.

She counted on it.

* * *

Tourists were scant from the view of El Castillo San Felipe del Morro. Marisol attributed the lack of interest to the time of the day and the rain. She was perfectly happy to be dry, looking out of the patio in the pleasant-temperature air conditioning of what was the late Luis Fernando's penthouse. A clock too utilitarian for a *narco* showed it was about an hour after midnight.

She wiped the blood off a blade usually used to peel limes. A hooker lay on the floor, having received a nonlethal blow to the larynx. Luis didn't have much of a throat anymore. Contents of his cut carotid artery left a large, growing stain on the carpet until his heart stopped pumping.

It was harder for Marisol to do than she thought. Not physically or emotionally, but she wasn't yet sure if killing Luis was practical. His answers from her interrogation made it feel better, but erstwhile protections were now up in the air.

After having snuck inside past security as a rich man's call girl, Marisol interrupted the boss and the girl-for-hire during a predawn fellatio session after having made her way inside the suite. She knocked the girl out, then gave a left jab to Luis's solar plexus.

The closest weapon was the paring knife. After having knocked him to the ground with a kick to the groin, she aimed and sliced his right distal biceps tendon. The savagery proved a useful intro to questioning.

Marisol had offered vodka from the minibar, being the closest antiseptic to her weapon. The prostitute's discarded pantyhose served as a temporary tourniquet, prolonging Luis's life long enough for her to play both good and bad cop. True information required at least some degree of trust, even if borne out of desperation.

Her late boss had confided that he'd allowed his own lesser thugs hit the spot where she'd been guarding their FBI hostage Lopez. Despite the wishes of de Salinas and the drugstore cowboy *gringo* representing Shelling-Polk Corporation, Luis had then called some *sicarios*, focusing on the one possible escape route for Marisol after rumors she was with the Fed.

The *narco* had sent the thugs to intercept them at Oscar's shack outside Bayamón, giving the order to kill anything that moved. With that, came his own death sentence. Marisol became the executioner when it became personal.

Luis's *cojones* hadn't shielded him when *la soldado* delivered an ultimate cut to his throat. He was a *pendejo* with no loyalty or honor, but she'd killed who might have had the potential to be useful. She lost her income. Honor and vengeance didn't provide her with income for food, shelter, or recreation.

It wasn't a complete strategic blunder, she reasoned. Marisol, *la soldado*, sent a message that everyone was vulnerable. The *gringo farmacéutico* and his FBI lapdog would face more risk now. She had a slight problem starting a war with a bunch of *pendejos* she didn't know, but she reasoned her actions would be more automatic in survival mode.

Before paying Luis the final visit. she had raided the location of where a MAC-10 automatic and extra magazine had been buried for when stealth and accuracy didn't matter as much. It was right after she left Agent Lopez asleep near the river.

Her one time hostage and captor was skilled at survival and knew how to get her off.

If her life had gone differently, they might have been an item. As it stood, she had decided to leave him to his own devices, justifying the distance as good both for him and her. Oscar was proof enough to sever ties with those she could rely on. She took the truck but ditched it once in the capital.

She had shit to do, and if she were to make ties with humanity, it would be more natural to do so for mutual benefit. The rationale helped her focus, despite an occasional barrage of questions that rattled through her head.

Was she an assassin. a survivor, or a soldier? Did she have the potential to be a protector? A lifesaver? Or was she only built for vengeance?

Marisol snagged a fifth of *ron anejo* before setting herself to lie low. Resources abounded, giving her a leg up.

Marisol didn't bother cleaning the scene before leaving. Since the late Luis Fernando's underlings didn't care enough to protect him, they wouldn't work too hard with *policía* to investigate his death. It was lonely toward the top tier of the underworld. A knock on the door to the penthouse made her nervous enough to reconsider her lack of housekeeping.

"Señor Fernando?" Jimmy Ocasio said on the other side. *"Todo bien?"*

Although the concern in the voice was unconvincing, Marisol didn't stick around. Knocks didn't need to grow more frequent and forceful for her to second guess her sudden split.

La soldado snuck out on the patio with rum, the release of killing someone, and an unlikely sense of freedom. A hop down to the dimly lit balcony below allowed her to make her way in an undetected exit.

19

Meet the New Boss, Same as ...

Russell Thurgood stubbed out a Cohiba and stood after a late breakfast of steak and eggs. He took ample time to enjoy the marble-lined, granite-tiled, chrome and brass-outfitted dining room of the condo the Shelling-Polk Corporation had arranged for him.

The usual nerves or hostility in his green eyes focused to pointed pupils when an assistant whisked away dishes and announced important visitors. He hoped for positive news after a messenger had reported earlier about Luis Fernando's mid-fellatio slaughter session.

The ripped-out throat was just another heap of fertilizer on the shit show that had been the last couple of days. His condo lay down the road from a row house he had used to hold Carey Riley in a basement. Assets were quick to become liabilities after her escape.

Some blocks away, off of Avenida José de Diego, tough guys on the late Luis Fernando's payroll had lost her among local college students, gaping tourists, and enterprising locals. Beside losing any leverage he'd had over Carey's tough guy husband, he had now lost the FBI agent, Lopez, after reports of drug gang gunfire from out of Santa Cruz.

With his local *narco* having bled out, Russell Thurgood reasoned he would have to take a more active role in the *narco* scene to launder funds and suppress locals. He hoped for any good news as corporate-subsidized servants picked out clothes fitting enough for Sunday at a Southern Baptist Convention service or casual enough for club seats at the El Paso rodeo.

"Thank God you beaners are better at working than you are at speaking American," he said to the man handing him a starched, white, button-down.

Thurgood put on khakis instead of jeans as he gave the house man a slanted smile and told him to get some booze. Politics and fake etiquette suited him better than work on the ground, despite the image he hoped to project. He slicked his sandy hair back as the help delivered a decanter of bourbon and two old fashioned glasses to a desk in a living area. The drugstore cowboy then gave the okay for his guests to enter.

Assistant Special Agent-in-Charge Rodriguo de Salinas entered in a tailored black suit, leading a muscled, caramel skinned tough guy whom Thurgood had recently seen as a member of Luis's detail. A server got another tumbler of whiskey after the boss nodded for it. Thurgood pointed at chairs opposite him before all three men took a seat.

"You've heard the news, I suppose," Agent de Salinas said, swirling his bourbon. "You need a new man in the field at your disposal while your accountants clean *narco*-dollars. Your glad-handing with Secretary Juan Ramón Sanchez-Riera keeps you from doing the day to day.

"Don't worry," he continued after Thurgood fidgeted with his hands and cracked his knuckles. "I have to stay above the fray as well, due to being FBI. That doesn't mean I don't know helpful resources."

The Fed introduced Jimmy Ocasio after Thurgood gave the nod to continue. He explained he was the former head of Luis Fernando's security. The late *narco* had countered de Salinas's wishes. So any dereliction of duty on the part of Luis's security was bought and paid for until a new employer could be found.

Ocasio was introduced as a useful tool with extensive experience as a private security contractor. A veteran of 2001's Operation Enduring Freedom and 2003's Operation Iraqi Freedom, the gun-for-hire could prove a linchpin for Shelling-Polk's ground operation success.

The job candidate, Ocasio, only nodded. He acted as an obedient soldier and prize bull for whoever was paying for the ring. After the okay, in turn, from the Thurgood and the Fed, the man brought out a Glock 19, field-stripped it, and cleaned and lubed its parts. Afterward, he looked for approval.

"Will this Spic work to increase my profit?" Thurgood asked the Fed. "No offense, Rodriguo, but I got to know if this fella can take orders and follow them."

Ocasio finally spoke, "What do you mean, sir? My family raised me in Durham, North Carolina, where I got my first real job catching wetbacks for a private security company. I came to Puerto Rico for the tax breaks."

Thurgood clasped his hands together and chuckled. De Salinas smiled with relaxed eyes as if a burden were off his back.

"Goddammit, you're hired son," Thurgood said. "Now let's get to brass tacks. What about your missing agent, Rodriguo? Carey and Ron are still in the wind. Luis's killer is out there, too. The game needs more finessing than when Luis could absorb any heat."

"Ignorance is innocence," De Salinas said after shooting his whiskey. "Municipal cops are looking in the neighborhoods for the assassin and the rogue FBI agent. So it will work out for the FBI and a mainland investor if we find ourselves in the position to take them down."

The Assistant Special Agent-in-Charge continued that the hardest target would be the Riley family. Ron was likely looking for allies. Luis had said something about a state policeman friendly with the *gringo*. The cop was noticed during the torching of the Fajardo house he, his wife, and their kid had shared.

Ocasio could be a good asset to neutralize Ron if the price was right.

"This all sounds fine and dandy," Thurgood said after a chuckle. "How many beaners can you and Ocasio round up to put boots on the ground?"

"How many do you need, sir?" Ocasio asked.

The three finished their whiskeys while the Shelling-Polk boss appeared to enjoy some control of strategy. Thurgood gained a penthouse at a mid-rise condo along Calle Norzagaray as an added part of the deal. It was adjacent to where Luis's throat had been slashed, so rent was a bargain for *gringos* who want to "live it up." The Fed and Ocasio left before Thurgood broke out the cocaine in celebration.

Breaking the law was part of the gig, one of the myriad ways the pharmaceutical executive found to unwind. Russell Thurgood's day was looking up.

* * *

The arid desert in Ron's mouth didn't make for a pleasant morning, even if it was a short one. The alarm from his Nokia around an hour before noon nudged him from barely unconscious to just awake. The monochrome, yellowish-backlit display told him he had a voice message. He punched in the four-digit code to hear the latest. The voice over the receiver jolted him awake.

Carey's voice struck him stronger than his last gulp of whiskey last night from a bottle of Jack he'd found in Carlos's cabinet. She apparently remembered the number of the burner he'd picked up outside a Pueblo Supermarket. The night he had come home to Fajardo to find her gone seemed so long ago.

He longed for her and listened as she explained she was safe, but on the run. Per her hints, he gathered she was headed south. They'd wanted to tour south on the PR-52 Highway with John in tow, but hadn't yet had the chance. She said she had started a late honeymoon without him.

The realization that Carey had fled from her escort alarmed Ron initially, but any worry subsided when he realized she had probably taken out two of Carlos's friends to "escape." Knowing her, she'd used nonlethal force to get her way. The memory of her curves stirred lascivious urges until the seriousness of their situation smacked his consciousness back to the present.

Ron pulled his well-worn, navy-colored cargo pants off a line he'd hung at Carlos's apartment the evening before. He'd washed them, a set of boxer briefs, socks, and a tank top in the kitchen sink after confirming a meeting with the *campesino* while enjoying his friend's whiskey. The current pounding in his head and obligations reminded him he wasn't in his twenties anymore, so he poured himself a bowl of Cocoa Puffs and gulped down a Good O Kola to get himself going.

He held off on adding any Jack to the Kola. He had shit to do.

His amigo, Carlos, had told him over the phone to travel south on the PR-52 for a meeting just north of Caguas. Ron was to wear Carlos's only *guayabera* shirt because the *campesino* contact, Willy Ortiz, liked to make fun of *gringos* who wore them.

From Carlos's assurances, insults were a small price to pay. This *cabrón,* Willy, wasn't someone to mess with. He harvested less legal products as well as lettuce, tomatoes, and tilapia, with other *campesinos* on a joint-owned aquaponic farm, Ecología. He was also a gun enthusiast in the vein of a more likable, leftist version of Ted Nugent.

Word was that Willy had an M2 Browning machine gun that he liked to shoot off from his mountain cabin. Carlos hadn't confirmed the rumor, not wanting to have to report it or cultivated cannabis to authorities.

Ron, happy to not have an official duty to the law, buttoned up a *guayabera*, grabbed his Beretta, checked it, and made his way to Carlos's Honda. He drove it southward from the apartment. He promised to pick up Carlos after meeting the notorious Willy Ortiz

At a casual pace after hitting the PR-52, Ron began to worry about his stepson. The foliage around the highway helped him relax, and he slowed before the asphalt curved and snaked through the peaks and valleys of Cordillera Central. He would have gone into vacation mode if people weren't trying to kill him and his family. He told himself to have faith in Margarita and her pump action shotgun.

Ron spotted a truck pulled off the side and slowed down further. Black smoke billowed from somewhere around the engine, while the bed appeared full of crates of produce. He noticed the name, "Ecología," stamped on the cab's door before he heard a pop in his Honda's front, passenger side tire. Ron's better judgment whispered that he ought to continue to the meet up with Willy, but unhealthy curiosity and the prospect of a damaged wheel rim prompted him to pull over.

There didn't appear to be anyone nearby nor any nefarious evidence about the nick to his tire. Ron figured doing a solid for one of Willy's farmers was a good idea so he hiked a short way north, back toward the truck wreckage. Perhaps he could get a hand with his tire. He was hoping for a win-win.

Ron realized he couldn't see any driver and grew astonished as the smoke died down, letting him get closer to the truck. He felt vulnerable with only his Beretta and his Nokia burner to help him. While on the driver side of the cab, a burlap sack put over his head soon cut off Ron's view of the world.

"*Oye hijo'e puta!*" Ron heard in an excited, bass voice before getting an injection. The chloral hydrate rushing through his arm was unnecessary, but he didn't waste his energy arguing. Unconsciousness extinguished both aggravation and light.

20

Huevos

Agent Lopez began to open his eyes, stopping his lids as they met a blindfold around his head. The familiar scent of burning wet hay invaded his nostrils, making him want a joint. From the remnants of light beyond his eyelids, he could tell he was likely above ground during the day. He was pretty sure it was later the same day he'd been knocked out south of Caguas. Waking up alone in a field near the Rio Turabo with only one's clothes was never a good omen despite a pleasant night before.

Earlier memories of his sleep in the tangle of Marisol's solid yet somehow soft arms made him feel let down in the present. He and *la soldado* had enjoyed their tryst, ending up in the bed of the commandeered Toyota Tacoma. Marisol and the Tacoma's absence early the morning after was somehow unsurprising, even if the hope was to awaken next to her.

At any rate, goons from the PR-52 had swarmed Lopez after getting off the highway from the north. Out of a Honda Ridgeline pickup, four stout, muscled *pendejos* charged him with semi-automatic tactical rifles. The tallest one couldn't have been over 5-foot-9, but the goons used firepower and strength in numbers to send him to a less peaceful unconsciousness.

In the present, Lopez figured he was in some other limbo like the one Marisol had guarded him in, but he ascertained he was in less competent hands this time. The *pendejos* holding him were more talkative, for one. They bitched and moaned more than any office flunkies back in San Juan FBI. He listened as they complained about the added guard duty along with the farm work.

Lopez's guards might have been weaker, but the lack of street noise and traffic made his circumstances more serious. With no ability to see or hear otherwise, Lopez surmised that he was both alone and away from civilization with no immediate transport. Also, his hands were zip-tied.

The scent of cannabis helped Lopez relax a bit more as he pieced together a plan. He figured his best play was to be a non-threatening pain in the ass when the time came. He waited for an opportunity to present itself.

Lopez suddenly heard a vehicle outside. Queen's "Another One Bites the Dust," echoed in the background as if from a bootleg cassette played over a pimped-out subwoofer. A new presence could be felt. Intuition hinted at a boss and a new captive.

Before the other captive was brought near him, Lopez was able to shrug his blindfold away with grimaces and winks. With an eye partially getting a view, he watched as a goon shoved the new prey to the floor. A dark-brown skinned man, whom Lopez supposed was the leader, soon delivered a kick to the goon's *cojones*. It was an immediate staff memo, showing the stakes with the steel toe of his boot.

"*Cuidado!*" the boss said.

The new hostage's hands were unbound, the only constraint was a sack blocking his sight. Apart from the recent slap, he was otherwise handled with hands of stitched silk. He was waking up at a gradual pace, working himself to his knees.

Lopez didn't get handled with the same kid gloves. He kept his eyes on the new visitor, hoping for an ally as the boss whispered in a guard's ear. He nodded when the thug asked the Fed if he could translate some phrases to English.

As the other captive began swaying to consciousness, the dark-skinned boss removed the hood and offered a swig from a bottle of Dasani. After blinking his eyes and subsequently vomiting on the ground, the pale-skinned prisoner rubbed his temples and looked around, less like a lost puppy than a pit bull getting ready to strike.

After viewing the boss and some of the muscle, the familiar-looking *gringo's* eyes flinched to Lopez. He spat a bile-filled puddle on the ground before blinking and readjusting his gaze to the man offering bottled water.

"Buenas tardes, Señor Riley," said the mahogany-skinned man-in-charge. *"Espero que el FBI pueda traducir. Mi ingles no es muy bueno."*

"The asshole holding us doesn't speak very good English," Lopez said after a smack to the back of his head. "So I translate, okay?"

The Riley *gringo*, still kneeling if unbound, listened and took in the entire scene. Lopez did the same, as well as he could.

The structure they were in was a large shed with wood slat walls and hardwood floor, its gray left-to-the-elements hue suggesting teak. The pair of windows on opposite walls showed palms and other green foliage in the distance.

Lopez and the other captive shared a look of recognition

before the *gringo* continued.

"*Eres grosero con un amigo de Carlos Velez,*" he said. "*Come mierda.*" There's no need to be rude when I'm on your side. Eat shit.

This prompted a laugh from the big man in charge. He shrugged his shoulders after the chuckle. The *gringo* was showing he was a tough guy who was blunt with words and disliked being dicked around.

The boss responded with a seemingly gentle cadence that bordered on being respectful.

"You were said to be a stubborn goat, *un cabrón,*" Lopez translated. "Willy, the big man here, says he wants to hear what you have to say. You are a pal to Carlos Velez, *sí*? He'll help you as long as you keep showing you have *cojones.*"

Riley returned a grin as Willy extended a right arm to help him stand. The muscled, dark-skinned Latino-in-charge hadn't expected the *gringo* to shift his weight to his left and use his right fist to punch a knee. All hell broke loose when sniper rifle fire struck from outside the shack.

The six stoned, sycophantic soldiers around the room, including one who'd been hassling Lopez, reacted too late. Two of six near the north side window dropped with bullet wounds through their foreheads. On the floor, Willy reached for the Desert Eagle handgun he had just dropped.

The cautiously handled captive, Riley, grabbed Willy's pistol before aiming it at the captor's newly submissive face. The barrel shifted from the mahogany-skinned man's left eye to his right. The four remaining guards, now prone, focused their aim toward the outside, per their more immediate interest.

The *gringo* was more in charge than anyone else. Lopez figured it was time to make an ally.

* * *

When sniper rounds had taken out two goons, Ron rushed to retake any control that'd been taken from him. He had recognized the FBI as the Latino last seen under automatic weapons fire of the jungle highway. The *pendejo*-in-charge, Willy Ortiz, was one of the *campesinos* who, though rarely showing up at El Rococo, often paid the tab.

Ron aimed his newly acquired Desert Eagle between the eyes of his wanna-be captor. Before more suppressed rounds made their way into the teak floor, he hit his captive in the jaw. It wouldn't help anyone to kill or debilitate Willy, and Ron took a glint of pleasure showing he was the boss.

From the periphery of his eyesight, Ron saw the four flunkies hit the ground as rifle rounds ripped through the air, having already killed two others. Urine leaked from the drawers at least one as another received a shot that ruptured through his hamstring. No femoral arteries appeared severed, which Ron appreciated. He crawled on knees and elbows to the familiar-looking fellow captive. Ron was more excited than worried that they always seemed to connect under heavy gunfire.

Ron removed the FBI man's blindfold and asked in Spanish if he wanted to live. He nodded and rattled on about Willy's sister along with the word *chinga*. It was a welcome response. They didn't have time to exchange wan grins as Ron used his hidden Schrade to cut the man's zip tie.

With Willy prostrate to the floor and his goons prone, shooting pistols to counter fire from outside, Ron and his accomplice hugged the ground and crawled toward the wall with the north side windows. They stayed out of the line of fire, using shadows to evade anyone's sights. Willy stayed near, to the rear of their evasive maneuvers.

Willy's whistle pierced the air amidst the ricocheted lead rounds. Anything targeted through the view of the north side windows was becoming as perforated as Swiss cheese. Ron and the FBI man gave a glance back to their onetime captor, who had hung back a few yards from the quick cadenced army crawl.

Willy pointed to a large trunk near him along the wall that measured two yards in length, giving a thumbs up and a wink. Ron pointed the barrel of the Desert Eagle in his direction and returned the wink, watching.

Even from the respectable distance between them and Willy, Ron could see the ivory eyes roll in the man's mahogany-skinned face as he mouthed the words *"no pendejo."* Willy raised the middle finger on his left hand in a universal salute before nodding north toward the windows. The eruption of rounds from outside was getting closer to the shack as Ron decided to trust the *Boricua,* giving a nod.

Willy returned a thumbs up, before pulling a pin that collapsed the trunk and opened up a small partition on the north wall. The rumored M2 Browning, fed by a belt of .50 caliber rounds, showed itself in its lethal beauty. Ron smiled as the barrel pointed north toward convening shooters.

"Vámonos!" Willy shouted before sliding his keys across the teak floor in a move Ron registered as unnaturally smooth. *"Llevese mi troca."*

"He wants us to take his truck," the FBI guy said.

"Vámonos!" Ron responded. He had to chuckle as he put the Desert Eagle in his rear waistband and nodded his accomplice to follow toward the exit. The toddler-like expression of joy on Willy's face reverberated in Ron's mind as .50 caliber rounds

quickly stopped any moron who was being paid to encroach on *la cabina*.

The rat-a-tat of the machine gun was a staple of war films and video games, but for Ron, it brought back memories from basic training to the sands of Mosul. M2 gunfire in Iraq was directed from radicalized insurgents and sectarian sociopaths to take advantage of local instability.

Ron had to quash his memories and his initial panicked reaction. In the present, the deadly barrel of the M2 was in the control of a more likable sociopath who shared an interest in staying alive and taking out *sicarios*. The gleeful look in the eyes of his new *amigo loco* also made the rat-a-tat more fun than a strobe light at a strip club. Worlds were colliding.

Rewarded for his trust in Willy, Ron realized any sputtering gunfire from outside the shack had become a moot point. There was no reason to worry about any attention to Ron and the FBI guy as they looked for their ride. Still moving in a crouch, Ron spotted the Honda Ridgeline, emptied of vegetables from its bed. Ron took the driver side and the other man took shotgun.

The two drove away with no words between them until the sound of the M-2 had faded.

"So, you speak English and can escape psychos with automatics in the rainforest," Ron said to the man. "Anything else I should know? *Como te llamas?* Can I trust you, for now?"

"I am called Roberto Lopez. I used to work for the FBI, but I'm not so sure now," his companion said, raising his palms. "As for trust, what choice we have, Señor Riley? *A mi, plín.* I don't care."

"Call me Ron."

Ron was happy to be in the company of Agent Lopez, whom

his pal Matt Russo had talked about. The newfound surrealism of forced trust and cooperation in the past hours told him he was on the right path. The nod and a wink over a Browning machine gun showed it was a brave new world. Laces of lightning spread out over the darkening horizon as the two found their way to the PR-52 and headed north.

As Ron rolled the window shut, Lopez nudged a cassette in the tape player, They both heard a cheesy baseline before Freddie Mercury's cunningly theatrical, overly happy, campy voice poured out of the speaker.

"Don't try suicide, nobody's worth it..."

Ron and his passenger chuckled. Adrenaline and a sense of humor helped power through exhaustion, dehydration, and alcohol withdrawal during the drive. They had to get in touch with Carlos and find a place to recharge.

21

Sirens

Remnants of daylight faded in the distant western horizon as Marisol drank water from the tap. She was in a flimsy flat on a nondescript *calle* in La Perla neighborhood of San Juan, a fitting nook in which to take a break after bumping off her boss. Travel guides and those with any official status were loathe to give the area attention due to its soiled reputation.

La soldado again found herself in the middle of a storm. As dark clouds shot forth rain from the sky, Marisol recalled the days' events and how she'd come to meet her new hosts, *una mujer y dos niños*. It started with two dirty cops, roughed up transients, and a kid caught in the middle.

Marisol had been walking along the wall of the historic slaughterhouse district earlier in the afternoon, trying to clear her mind with the ever-present rumble of the Atlantic against the nearby shore. Outside the flat, a duo of *policía municipal* de San Juan was harassing a couple of drifters in an alleyway blocked off by an out-of-place Ford Falcon. She saw a cop punch a man in the stomach before a young boy wandered into the alley and faced the dangerous end of a Smith & Wesson.

Faced with threats to a kid, Marisol did what any recently unemployed soldier would do if burdened with an ax to grind and a freshly ignited spark of ethics. She retrieved the loaded MAC-10 from a sack on her back, entered the alley, pointed the barrel at *la policía*, and asked if they felt lucky. Out-gunned, the two cops raised their hands and retreated to the Falcon. Anyone involved decided to keep things copacetic, and Marisol took the boy back to his guardian.

A sense of safety was what she offered the woman her age and two elementary school-aged boys in exchange for the opportunity to stay with them for an evening at their ground floor flat. The ramshackle, red-painted floors above them barely stood on wood-studded walls that held up a roof replete with rotting terracotta tiles. Marisol made her case for being protective with the automatic firepower at her side and the kid's observations. His word no doubt sealed the deal.

La soldado turned bodyguard-for-hire chopped her chestnut locks to a pixie cut that matched her petite, athletic physique. The cut served to cool her head and add a slim layer of anonymity. It helped to change appearances in her line of work.

Her new flatmates had used charcoal in a barrel outside to barbecue discarded ham hocks. Along with a bite of food, the woman provided her with a magenta-colored, flared skirt that danced above her knees.

Marisol politely declined the off-the-shoulder, cream-colored peasant top in favor of her tan tank top undershirt, being more practical. She had washed it earlier in the day in the sink of a public restroom. It was still damp, not that it mattered with her sweat in the tropical heat.

Awhile after dinner, the woman and the boys, who were

discovered to be nephews, got ready for slumber. The boy Marisol had protected gave *la soldado* a hug before he and the other one went to cots.

The guest and protector removed her skirt, her hips covered by a pair of boxers, as she found a guest blanket near the hot plate and sink that made up the family's kitchen. She relocated to rest in the adjacent dining and living room.

Marisol's thoughts ran to her tryst with the FBI man Lopez, a severing of ties, and how she found herself after helping a family in La Perla. Despite her lack of gainful employment, estrangement with normal life, and her human and inhuman actions from the past days, she found herself happier than she had been in a while. *Quid pro quo* felt better with some sense of ethics.

Marisol focused on her thoughts as the Atlantic crashed on the northern coast and exhaustion slowly crept over her. Her second to last thought before slumber flinched back to Luis's dying face. She was glad to have killed the *pendejo*. The surrounding air and resignation over Luis allowed her sinewy body relax

Her last thought was on Lopez, faintly hoping he was not too angry for how she left him. He could make her tic but thought it best to leave him out of what she had to do.

In time, peace reclaimed her and the homey hovel where she hid.

* * *

Thunder erupted in Carey's ears after twilight as she pulled the Mustang into a parking lot at the Plaza Cayey Walmart Supercenter. She didn't relish the idea of shopping or speaking with strangers. She was hungry and tired after leaving jail, breaking free of *la policía*, and stealing a fine rental automobile from tourists.

Carey had $80 to spend from looting the cops. She'd dig into the wallets of the tourists if it became necessary, unsure of where to send reimbursement since she'd left their passports. If she found herself on the right side of the law again, an anonymous drop-off might be arranged for the authorities.

The first thing to do was swap cars, and the thunderstorm and darkened evening sky helped her maintain stealth. Carey hadn't much experience with grand theft auto outside adventures in the Chicago suburbs with the man who became her husband.

She allowed herself a few moments to dwell on her boys before eyeing a patsy. It was an easy mark. As she pulled near a disabled parking spot where a Toyota Camry with standard plates was illegally parked, she rationalized that she was delivering karma.

In the back seat of the Camry, a caramel-skinned toddler and his primary school-aged sister busied themselves. The ignition was turned on and the engine was running in neutral, the parking brake engaged. No parents were around until Carey jimmied open the driver side and got behind the wheel.

Carey backed up the Toyota and replaced it with the Mustang. After shutting the stolen rental off and wiping any of her fingerprints, she led the kids to their new back seat. She left the keys on the pavement next to the driver side door. The tourists' wallets lay on the passenger side floor.

Once finding a spot on the other side of the parking lot for the Camry, Carey went to the store with her money and some change. From a pay phone in the entrance, she called *la policía* to report the stolen Mustang, giving the rental's license plate and description. She felt bad for the two kids, but a distraction outside wouldn't hurt as she went into the store and got supplies

Within a fifteen minutes, Carey emerged with beef jerky, applesauce, a sleeping bag, sunscreen, a Nokia burner with minutes, a half-dozen bananas„ a large bottle of water, a number of full-sized bags for waterproofing, a new T-shirt, boxers, some running shoes, a new pair of cargo shorts, and bug spray. She was out of cash when she left the store where people are supposed to "save money, live better." "Living better" was a relative idea, but she had gained some necessities.

While *la policía* showed up to check on the stolen Mustang with a parking violation, life was decidedly not better for the lady who was called to the car. Carey would have chuckled had she not seen the scared faces of her kids in the backseat. Her disposition didn't lighten when the lady threw a punch toward a cop, was handcuffed, and put in the back of a cruiser. Life for the kids would be harsh either way, she reasoned.

After returning to her newly acquired Toyota, Carey casually left the parking lot and headed north back toward Caguas. There were more places to pull off the PR-52 and relax in anonymity there. She found a side route to a deserted area that would serve her needs.

In the space, she took care of basic hygiene, put down the seats, changed to the boxers and T-shirt and stretched out the sleeping bag. Carey opened the water bottle and munched on the beef jerky, trying to calm herself. With her body supine, eyes toward the sky out of the passenger side window, thoughts of Ron and John swirled in her mind as the sound of cicadas lulled her to sleep.

22

Macho Men

In the morning, Russell Thurgood took in the view from his new penthouse of a mid-rise off of Calle Norzagaray. He gazed toward El Castillo San Felipe del Morro in the short distance, displeased with developments over the last couple of days. He exhaled a puff of smoke from his Cohiba as his mind wandered to what had gone wrong. A swirl of Rémy Martin around his tongue failed to sweeten the bitter residue from recent setbacks or his espresso.

The next notch of never-do-well was the unsuccessful attack on an insurgent farmer's hideout in the Cordillera Central mountains. Convenient for Thurgood, compromised cops who'd owed Special Agent de Salinas a favor were among the scattered and the dead from the attack. Observations had put Ron Riley and an FBI straggler fleeing amid the chaos.

The results weren't a matter of public knowledge, at least for now. None of the casualties were particularly loyal or knowledgeable of Shelling-Polk's machinations. The *cojones* of the resistance *campesinos* was almost enough to make him laugh. Reports of his goons fleeing M2 fire amused him more than it should have.

Thurgood's guys and *narco* allies had been watching the *campesino,* Willy Ortiz, for a while because of the man's "anti-corporate, anti-colonialism" stance. Possession of the M2 had been a rumor until now, and though it commanded respect, Shelling-Polk's local help would have to do more legwork.

Recent news then came in about push back in nearby La Perla.

Municipal police pals on payroll looking to get tough with locals reported resistance in an alley and were waiting for instruction on how to respond. A Latina with a MAC-10 had ordered his men to stand down. Her petite, sinewy build and uncommonly feminine, if fatal, good looks told Thurgood his police goons might have run into someone he'd heard about. Luis mentioned an explosive firecracker he'd employed until a few days before his throat was slashed.

"I reckon we're on the tail of a hen looking out for someone else's brood," he said to Jimmy Ocasio. "The queen bitch is probably responsible for bumpin' off your late boss, Luis. Since city police were threatened, budding business interests are entitled to respond in kind."

Thurgood by no means practiced Santeria, but he felt events were conspiring with some sort of cosmic force. He was happy his FBI man had introduced Ocasio to tie up loose ends and extend entanglements with locals for the Shelling-Polk Corporation. Having his contacts with his Luis's former army helped align the stars in his own mind. He didn't mind disposing federal subsidies to local thugs.

On the rebound from letting his old boss die, Ocasio knew better than to let his new host know what kind of parasite he was: a well-trained one whose loyalty went to bidders with backing. Funding from legitimized mainland interests made him a dangerous asset.

Luis's former security head was quick to present a disposable crew from local talent. Anyone calling shots in the penthouse or barking orders expected events to get messy. Gathered muscle didn't need to be the best and brightest to make noise.

The disruption team had five former enforcers of Luis Fernando, with a breadth of experience from low-level smack-slinging to kidnapping. Thurgood was happy to delegate Ocasio to give orders and arm the team. Shelling-Polk could maintain plausible deniability if "any civies should need to meet their God."

The team armed themselves with various semi-automatic pistols. All were directed to defend themselves by any means necessary, should they feel their lives were in jeopardy. Three enforcers took Honda CBR motorcycles to head just east. The two others followed in a Dodge Charger. They'd all stocked up on extra magazines.

Any official credentials weren't explicitly tied to Shelling-Polk. Any bloodshed could be spun as gangs taking advantage of a law enforcement vacuum. Neither Ocasio nor Thurgood cared too much whether the team had casualties. Expendable thugs were cheaper than well-connected defense lawyers.

On a more official note, Thurgood had unpaid Shelling-Polk Corporation interns monitor police radios around the island. After *una gringa* reportedly hijacked *dos uniformados* in Trujillo Alto, unexpected broadcasts followed about a Walmart in Cayey Plaza. A stolen rental Ford Mustang was found from an anonymous call to authorities.

The alleged Mustang thief raved about losing her Toyota Camry after her arrest. Ocasio was intuitive enough to connect some dots but smart enough to allow Thurgood to take credit.

The *gringo*-in-charge had friendly *policía* call for an APB on the Toyota with a description of Carey, knowing he could more easily take advantage of official channels to restore order. Coincidences along the PR-52 prompted him to make them look for patterns.

Thurgood's contacts with local politicos and *policía* enabled him as much as his use of the late Luis Fernando's thugs. He trusted his man, Ocasio, to deliver retribution on so-called threats to progress. Federally subsidized numbers guys laundered dirty money in the suites on the building level beneath him.

The drugstore cowboy pressed his Cohiba into the balcony railing before sitting his large behind in a chair and looking north on the Atlantic horizon toward Florida. A server soon set out a breakfast of steak and eggs, with Heinz ketchup that he eventually soaked up with warm tortillas. He awaited news from enforcers, cops, discreet accountants, and dealers about extending drug contracts.

A local call girl soon arrived to help bathe and entertain him until late morning. Thurgood didn't expect any backtalk or further impediments to his goals and wants. Considering the setbacks from the last few days, his optimism was either foolhardy or well bought and paid for.

La chica knew how to handle her audience, shedding shapely shorts and a camisole before drawing Thurgood's attention to more sensual sensations to the south. His hubris still haunted any harmony he should have been hunting in the present.

* * *

Under the same rays from the morning sun, Ron Riley exhaled and thought before he gulped the coffee that came with his San Juan hotel room. The coffee made Ron's stomach growl, but the complimentary caffeine was still better than Good O Kola.

The previous evening had been busy. After he and Agent Lopez had picked up Ron's buddy Carlos from a different hotel in the capital city, they lost the Honda pickup. The three checked into a Best Western under Carlos's ID. The state policeman, *el uniformado,* was the one guy who officially wasn't in trouble yet.

After having had a good laugh from Carlos about the encounter with Willy, Ron gave intel on Russell Thurgood, courtesy of his own observations and research from his pal in Miami. Agent Lopez added his thoughts on local corruption and hinted at the growing mistrust of his superior, Assistant Special Agent-in-Charge Rodriguo de Salinas. They had toasted with *ron añejo* in the hotel bar with the resignation to get to it in the morning.

From the small balcony, Ron smiled at the still-sleeping bodies of his two accomplices. The man who'd once abducted him to the jungle and flipped him the bird rather than speak English proved to be reliable. The one cop whom Ron trusted, Carlos, showed he had good allies, whether or not they came off as rough during first impressions.

In the orange hue of daylight, Ron missed his wife and worried about his son, but he considered the men sharing his nondescript hotel room good allies against a hegemonic, corrupt force. At least neither one had shot at him yet.

Los del Rio's "Macarena" made noise on Carlos's iPhone. Ron shook his head and returned inside to the groggy *unifor-*

mado. As he still was not completely sure how to answer the damn thing, he flicked the cop's ear and held what he guessed was the receiver to it.

"*Oye, chingado pendejo!*" Carlos erupted to his roommate's shit-eating grin before extending a middle finger salute. His apology to whoever was on the other end was calmer in Spanish too quick for the *gringo*.

Ron got the Fed and the cop cups of the complimentary coffee as Lopez began to stir. He didn't know how else to be useful. No one beside Carlos had access to a means of communication, whether it be a phone, a small computer, or an i-whatever-the-hell-it-was.

Ron handed Lopez a coffee, receiving a respectful nod before placing Carlos' cup on a bedside table and going to take a leak. He picked up bits and pieces for translation, noticing from the tone of voice alone that they were about to be in a rush. Nothing else was to be expected.

Carey had escaped cops and a leftist, *campesino* gun nut named Willy Ortiz had lit up an otherwise natural oasis in the Cordillera Central. It didn't take a genius or a translator to figure out there'd be more noise. The worry made Ron feel alive. Word of narco thugs in La Perla put the action on his, *el uniformado's*, and the Fed's radar.

The adrenaline and purpose of preparing for combat pumped through his veins. He had left the Army honorably, but it never left him. He melted away memories of Mosul to focus on the tasks at hand. A familiar conviction to complete the mission with his fellow Jawas had prepared him to fight against dicks who threatened his wife and child. A few splashes of water to his face and an emptied bladder helped him get his shit together.

Both his *amigos* were up and getting ready to leave. Within ten minutes, they'd all used the water closet, had raided pastries from the complimentary continental breakfast, and had gotten in an older model state police squad car.

From the Best Western parking lot, Carlos quickly got on the PR-17 and headed north toward La Perla. Ron and Lopez listened as he informed them about what was going on per police chatter. Ron checked his Desert Eagle and Lopez checked a Glock 26 subcompact supplied from *el uniformado*'s backup.

Carlos spoke of mercenaries taking advantage of *Boricuas* with little means to protect themselves. Sightings of muscular, well-armed *narco pendejos* ricocheted from *los calles*. In a way, all three *amigos* were expecting and looking forward to a fight. It wasn't a long ride to the action.

23

La Piña Está Agria

Marisol awoke to the sound and smell of beans, rice, and garlic sizzling in a pan in the red-painted La Perla flat where she had found refuge. The lard and chili powder-seasoned dish was a staple to *la mujer y dos niños*. Marisol's sharp instincts took over at the sound of pimped-out Honda motorcycle engines interrupted the delicious-sounding splatter.

Her eyes adjusted to the sliver of sunlight filtering through shut blinds as she grabbed the MAC-10 and stood, shushing her host with a slender finger to her lips. The *mujer* shut the hot plate off and shuttered her nephews into the water closet toward the rear of the flat.

With innocents safe enough, *la soldado* took her loud, if inaccurate machine pistol to the front facade to get a glimpse outside of what they faced. What she saw made the hair on the nape of her neck stand. The aggressors were making no attempts to keep operations on the down-low, making their firearms visible while pressuring bystanders. The ham-handling wasn't enough to throw her off balance.

Marisol would have preferred a more accurate rifle, and

better yet, a suppressor to conceal her position. She was still thankful to have the firepower needed to give a scare. She aimed with the care she could afford and shot one of the Hondas' rear tires. One of the men pissed his pants and the other two dove through shop windows for cover. Follow-up shots at the pisser's thigh ruptured a femoral artery. The other two exchanged cadenced semi-automatic fire toward her position.

La soldado was pleased to deal with a challenge, returning a short snap of automatic fire from her single position with inflamed, if not precise, passion. She flashed her teeth as they shot back, smiling with a rush as pistol fire glanced the wall little more than six inches from her head.

Within minutes, a Dodge Charger came in with reinforce-ment. Ensuing shots from the MAC-10 in Marisol's hands put holes the car. Her aim at the windows knocked them out, as well. She only had another burst or two of ammo left and realized she'd only kicked the hornet's nest.

"Coño."

Fire from four firearms convened on the rotting wood panels keeping Marisol and her recently adopted family from death. A crash from beyond the shack's walls changed the equation. A state police squad car stopped after having cracked the rear of the Dodge.

With a glance outside the window, she observed her three welcome visitors. After exiting the driver side with too little caution, *un uniformado* took a semi-automatic round to the chest, knocking him to the ground. A likely flak jacket underneath his blues allowed him to continue breathing and writhe with vigor.

From behind of the passenger side front door, a *gringo* with a handgun returned fire through an open window. Expert eruptions from his hand cannon took out one shooter from the Dodge with a quick blast to center mass.

Another arrival, the man she'd tried to kill a few weeks ago and then slept with outside Caguas the night before, backed up the *gringo*. After the three arrivals averted further staccato semi-automatic rounds, Roberto Lopez shot the other guy from the Charger in the side of the head when it lay exposed in the door frame.

As *el uniformado* called for backup and protected himself from further injury, the *gringo* and the Fed volleyed fire with the two remaining shooters. The motorcyclists focused fire toward Lopez. Fate put the agent in the hands of a guardian angel with a machine pistol.

Marisol shot the remaining rounds of the MAC-10 toward where the other motorcyclists hid. Through squinting eyes, she aimed at whichever speck of target showed through shop windows. Any fire from the cop car, compounded with hers, eventually silenced all signs of aggression. In time, the cop, the *gringo,* and her recent lover stopped shooting.

Marisol made the decision to split. The state police officer would soon have backup. With quiet from lack of gunfire, she rushed toward the kitchen of her hideout, kissed the *mujer* on the cheek and patted the *niños* on the head before heading through the back door. She found herself on the run again.

An explosion and a slew of shots from the front of the flat made her fear she'd fled too quickly. Her recent hosts were still vulnerable and she couldn't know if the FBI man, Lopez, was okay. A budding sense of empathy jolted her system more than any of the gunfire had.

Marisol shook her head and kept running. Before survival

mode completely kicked in, she allowed curiosity and a sliver of compassion inform her actions. She retraced a path to the flat to see if her hands, capable of killing and, as more recently discovered, kindness, could help in a desperate situation.

* * *

Despite rattled senses from an explosion near the La Perla flat, Ron and Lopez raced to check on Carlos. *El uniformado* had the instinct to survive despite a shot that almost penetrated his Kevlar. As the three *amigos* recovered and took stock of the situation, they realized one of the Honda motorcyclists had escaped their grasp. A shout from inside the flat soon materialized as a blast from a past.

Ron drew his Desert Eagle on the familiar-looking *mujer* he had seen at his bartender job at El Rococo before going on the run. She approached the three without a firearm. Her hands were raised toward the sky, empty palms up.

What surprised him more than her hints of familiarity and passivity was when Lopez shouted Ron down and ran to the woman. The rogue FBI agent stopped in front of her, his sidearm down. The world stood still when Lopez looked impassively as if he wasn't sure whether to be pleased or not. Drops of sweat ran off Ron's face

La soldado made the first move. As Carlos and Ron stood rigid, she hopped on Lopez, legs soon circling above his waist. The FBI man returned kisses given to him, bringing tension, if not weirdness, down a dozen notches or so.

El uniformado and the *gringo* tilted their heads in joint curiosity until their fellow survivor gave them a blushed grin that reddened his otherwise caramel-colored cheeks. All wasn't right with the world, but what are you supposed to do when two killers exchange kisses through dimple-pocked grins?

Lopez explained to Ron within the minute that the woman was *la soldado* from the rainforest. Apparently, this knowledge was meant to put Ron at ease.

"*Manos,*" Lopez said, "meet Marisol. She is really sorry for threatening us earlier, Ron. But she good people. We no choose who we can trust. Plus, she say she very happy to not have killed you or me."

Marisol gave three short whistles before two boys emerged from the flat. She whispered in Lopez's ear before he related to Carlos and Ron that the flat's residents could be good witnesses against the dead men in the street. Their aunt, the boys' guardian, had been abducted before *la soldado* had the chance to intervene.

Ron, Carlos, and Lopez found out more from innocent bystanders about whatever the hell was going on. The weapons, vehicles, and utter chutzpah of the shootout hinted at a backer with deep pockets. At least one US mainland *gringo,* Russell Thurgood, was in the crosshairs.

Ron chuckled to himself before *la soldado*, Lopez, and he tended to Carlos and wounded witnesses, giving first aid. They all figured they needed a plan as the *calle* began to return to normal despite the cracked cruiser, the shot-up Charger, the empty motorcycles, and four dead bodies. Police backup that Carlos had called would eventually show up. Ron and his new FBI pal needed to be gone at that point.

Necessity and clear heads made planning easier. Police chatter sounded over a speaker setting on Carlos's iPhone about door-to-door searches in Fajardo. The searches could lead to knowledge that John was hiding with Margarita.

Pause about his wife and son's safety fired between Ron's neurons quicker than any remaining adrenaline. His Army experience had formed a lesson to never underestimate forces opposing him. Ron asked Lopez to accompany him to Fajardo. The Fed was more fit to get physical.

With the task at hand for Ron and Lopez, the FBI man asked *la soldado* to accompany Carlos. It was safer for *el uniformado* to not cross the line into vigilantism, at least not actively. He could look the other way, should the soldier slip his custody to work outside the system.

Carlos could make official inquiries as to the whereabouts of Shelling-Polk Corporation's Russell Thurgood. Marisol's presence could help secure the safety of *los niños* who had helped her. Both sides of the law could be worked to do right by the boys' aunt.

"Thurgood and Shelling-Polk have a history of exploiting the innocent," Ron said. "You gotta sometimes work from the inside to fight the power. Sound right, Carlos?"

Carlos gave a wink and a nod. He could be counted on to bend the word of the law on occasion in the pursuit of real justice, and he knew he'd survive and be able to help best as an officer of the state police.

The soldier probably didn't have an official criminal record. Even if she did, intelligence on the ground took precedence over a shady past when it came to pressing police priorities.

After a quick discussion, the four operators, linked through fascination, friendship, duty, or some combination thereof, agreed to the plan. The two boys from the flat were willing to play their part.

Ron felt alive after escaping another shootout. Prospects

were difficult with one of the aggressors getting away from the scene, thanks to the explosion. The possibility of John being vulnerable clarified his mission. He would kill anyone who threatened his son, his wife, or Margarita.

Ron and Lopez took the two Honda CBRs that survived the explosions and gunfire. They rode east to intercept foreseen hostilities.

State police soon arrived to pick up Carlos, Marisol, and the two witnesses. *El uniformado* told Ron that his immediate coworkers were scrupulous enough to assist him with keeping innocents safe and assets in play.

24

The Pineapple is Sour

Carey had taken her time with the Toyota Camry along PR-52, using a roundabout route north because it was more familiar. After taking the PR-66 and the PR-3, Carey followed a number of streets to get to the Fajardo beach house she'd shared with Ron and John. Her husband hadn't had the chance to inform her that it had burned to the ground.

She'd been alert with occasional police sirens and other signs of the authorities, but the ruins where what had been her home renewed a sense of paranoia. She drove to a nearby side street, parking the Camry among other sedans, hoping to blend in as she turned on the radio to hear any news items.

From WTRU, an NPR station based in San Juan, she learned about a recent shootout in La Perla. The casualties included four yet-to-be identified men. Chosen eyewitness accounts hinted at drug gangs. Among those reportedly involved at the scene were Officer Carlos Velez and two bystanders, who'd taken off after assisting him. A woman was missing and two children were in custody of state police and emergency services.

Bewilderment and a need for answers clouded Carey's mind as the broadcast was interrupted by the just audible sound of sirens. She ditched the car, using a plastic Walmart bag to carry her essentials. She figured correctly that there was an APB on the Camry.

From a few blocks away, Carey crept near the yellowish, rusted trailer where her friend, Margarita, lived. She considered asking for a nondescript place to lie low and collect her thoughts. She instantly changed her mind as she surveyed the area from a distance, witnessing John playing outside before being ushered inside. Margarita held a shotgun with one hand, pointing it to the ground while taking John's hand with the other to head inside.

The sight made Carey's heart vacillate between bursting with joy and breaking with longing. The lioness wanted so badly to run to her son but knew she had to keep her distance as hyenas circled. Held back tears fueled renewed rage as she headed in the opposite direction on foot from her friend, her son, and the sound of sirens. She kept her eyes out for a new vehicle, clutching her goods and otherwise trying to blend in. Within a half hour, opportunity sputtered her direction.

A man straddling a Suzuki GSX proved her easiest prey when he cat-called before accelerating his two wheels from behind her, looking for a reaction. She gave him one, shaking her curvy hips and blowing a kiss.

The cycle squealed to a stop a couple hundred yards ahead before the prey made a right turn to come back around. She waited, bending at the waist, and releasing her bag after palming the Glock she'd taken from *la policía*. Soon-to-be kinetic energy stored itself in her thighs.

"*Aye, mami,*" the idiot said after returning within a yard from her side. He wore no helmet to protect from further brain damage. *"Quieres mi polla?"*

Carey returned a smile, baring her teeth in a way meant to hide rage and sadness beneath the surface. The contours of her body lulled him into a false sense of security. She noticed he had shifted the motorcycle to neutral before lunging at the loser to knock him and the Suzuki to the ground. She tucked and rolled back on her feet before closing the gap.

The Glock in her right hand made an audible thud with his unprotected brow. The muscles in her thighs then righted the bike with the speed of a machete chopping sugar cane, and she leveled the barrel her gun to his forehead. The cat-caller's pleas further reduced her willingness to pull the trigger.

Carey was far from a natural killer, and the puddle of urine spreading from the rider's pants to the asphalt put her role in perspective. In her past life as a stripper at a shack between Chicago and Naperville, she was lauded for having the allure of a naughty tutor. Teaching lessons was a role she embraced more freely than an assassin, especially when it came to *chicos* who needed manners.

Carey pointed the gun at the *pendejo's* head while striking the heel of her foot near his crotch.

"Di que lo sientes como lo dices a tu madre," she said. "I may not be your mother, but I hold your life in my hands as she did. Now, what would you like to say? *Qué te gustaría decir?"*

"Lo siento, señora," the cat-caller said. *"Por favor, no me molestes.* You take Suzuki?"

After readjusting the pistol to point at the man's *cojones*, Carey instructed him to fetch her Walmart bag. With a halted gait, he complied, handing over supplies. She put the burner phone, applesauce, and a banana in her cargo pockets, before telling the *pendejo* to get back on the ground, chest to the pavement.

She tossed the sleeping bag on him with her left hand, cradling the motorcycle with her legs before she switched the safety on her gun and stowed it in a pocket. Her bug spray can made a thud with the blanket-covered pervert before the Suzuki headed south on a roundabout loop toward the capital.

In a few hours, Carey planned to get in touch with Ron's acquaintance, Officer Carlos Velez. After arriving in the capital city, she parked the motorcycle and walked a few blocks.

Her mission was to stay as incognito as she could while heading to the San Juan Community Library. She needed a safe place to do some research and think before the evening would call her to inevitable action.

* * *

Russell Thurgood paced his recently acquired penthouse, ignoring the sight of countrymen snapping photos with camera phones at El Castillo San Felipe del Morro. His nose dripped from an afternoon snack of cocaine, champagne, caviar, and cilantro-laden calamari. Delicacies failed to lighten his mood.

Lack of success in his ham-fisted campaign of the day to quash trouble in La Perla proved ineffective. Luis's death made it more difficult for Thurgood to control local criminals and the "beaner's" killer would probably come gunning for him. He spat on the carpet, his head swirling at the setbacks before he shot another whiskey and took stock of assets and liabilities.

Thurgood worried about Ron's wife, Carey. Further pernicious probes found another way to keep Carey and Ron vulnerable. Interns scanning police chatter and government records revealed the Rileys had a son.

Follow-up canvassing in the area where Carey had last been seen revealed a pale-skinned brat of about four years staying with an older woman living in a basic yellow trailer. Police in Shelling-Polk's pocket hadn't harassed the boy and his local caretaker yet, but he'd be remiss if he didn't put pressure on whom he assumed was Carey and Ron's son.

The US mainland government supported him for now and he had a small collective of *narcos* who weren't beholden to public knowledge or interest. Thurgood also had his recent hire, Jimmy Ocasio, directing local talent. The general-discharged veteran had already proven to be useful enough.

For the attack on La Perla, Ocasio had set up an explosive with one of the enforcers on a Honda CBR motorcycle. After a slowdown in gunfire, the explosion allowed the man to threaten the woman and the kids who'd harbored a combatant. The late enforcer failed to take them out, however, only delivering the *mujer* to use as a hostage.

Ocasio put a suppressed round between his eyes. The outcome may have been different, had the other four been able to join him. Hostages had proven too much of a hassle. Ocasio's eye for economic risk-management made him move on after knocking the *mujer* unconscious, sticking a needle in her arm, and dumping her in an alley near el Museo de Arte y Historia de San Juan.

While currently in Thurgood's presence, Ocasio let the man vouching for his paycheck play enraged *gringo* politico. For what he was being paid from US mainland benefactors, he awaited his next orders. He was too well-compensated a tool to get hung up on a sense of duty to anyone, save himself.

"I require one response to threats to freedom, whether they be from nukular-armed thugs, hajis with rocks, or Mexican gorillas with guns," Thurgood said with a slur that was becoming more noticeable. "I expect you'll find the right way to respond, won't you, Ocasio? Hell, that's what I use federal dollars to pay you for. Ain't that right?"

"Well, like a water moccasin after a beaver, or a rooster after a grub, we'll do best if we know what we're after," Ocasio responded with a twang to play along. Like Thurgood, he knew how to downplay self-interest with good Christian, folksy ethos.

"I'm not usually keen on putting women folk in the line of fire, but it might be the best way to trap militants," Ocasio continued. "If we lean on this Margarita and John character, it's likely we'll be smacking a bull on the horns. Most folks don't like it, but you gotta fight fire with fire to ensure peace and prosperity from insurgents who want neither."

Thurgood took in his underling's pontification, impressed.

"We're called by our maker to protect against the enemies of America's advancement," he replied, hoping to save that quote for a campaign speech or future Fox Business interview. "We may have to grind some stones to lay the concrete of peace and prosperity. Godspeed, Ocasio. Be sure to keep me abreast of developments."

"Yes, sir," Ocasio responded. Despite thoughts of taking over the entire enterprise of Shelling-Polk Corporation as a more capable captain, he didn't fight being put in his place. He didn't have to justify his actions or deliver pliable political platitudes to the public or their representatives. It was a favorable trade-off for having a boss.

Thurgood observed his asset command recruits to hit Margarita's trailer. Ocasio called for smoke bombs and M84 stun grenades before any gunfire. If the situation got real, fire from heavier weapons could be justified. Goons had been weeded out if they had any qualms with following orders.

Ocasio considered the contingency that his targets might get help. If he'd learned nothing else as a soldier, it was to never underestimate the opposition. He reiterated that point for his team. The four chosen goons figured their armaments were overkill to take a hag and a four-year-old, but they listened intently on rules of engagement.

"We're to take the female and the juvenile in for questioning," Ocasio said. "Only use non-lethal ordinance against the two. As other actors may threaten the rule of law or pose risks to the safety of yourselves or civilians, you have heavy arms at your disposal."

Ocasio then repeated the orders in Spanish.

Two dishonorably dismissed cops and two private security/low level drug dealers hopped into an armored Hummer with the non-lethal deterrents and other weapons. One of the thugs riding shotgun had an AR-15; the other three had Glock 18 automatic handguns. They nodded to Ocasio before heading en route to the Fajardo.

Thurgood had sobered up with espresso as the sun revolved out of the western horizon from his view on the penthouse balcony. He lit another Cohiba as he called his communications guy to help figure out how to deal with the media in the face of any further disruption on the ground.

He put a lot of trust in Ocasio, who took a command post alongside guarded money launderers in an office suite located lower in his building. Ocasio would be on the comms and calling shots on the ground with an ear toward keeping the boss safe.

The *gringo*-in-charge tilted his cowboy hat at the last glimmer of the sun's rays. He longed for peace of mind or at least normalization of his greed. It might prove to be a long night, but he had an experienced team in place and didn't consider excessive pride a fatal flaw.

25

Lioness

Marisol sat in the rear seat of the police cruiser as Carlos Velez rode shotgun and chatted with the patrolman behind the wheel. Before she and her friendly Fed had gone separate ways, Lopez urged her to work with Officer Velez to protect innocent lives. She hoped any newfound sense of compassion and camaraderie wouldn't go to waste as the car headed to the state police station at Avenida Roosevelt. Twilight approached.

Traffic along the PR-1 south moved with the speed of a tortoise, which didn't help anyone feel relaxed. Marisol looked ahead with unease as an ambulance ahead of them carried the boys who had helped her.

La soldado reassured herself that Officer Velez was an ethical man of duty. His actions spoke loudly to assuage her usual skepticism. Carlos had looked *los medicos* in the eye, reciting their badge numbers, before entrusting them to head further south to the San Juan City Hospital with *los niños*. A sense of trust was as odd for her as any empathy she'd found.

Marisol resigned to herself to be a work in progress.

An awakened humility and vulnerability harvested in

Marisol's mind. She considered the lack of handcuffs and unlocked back door to be good signs. Remaining unarmed was a difficult concession, but one she knew was needed. With her sinewy body and feline eyes on a caramel face, she reminded herself that she had other tools beside high-powered guns.

With muscular legs crossing under the magenta skirt and chestnut strands of hair brushing her dimples, Marisol smiled in the rear-view mirror as the patrolman driver locked eyes with her. Conversation halted between him and Officer Velez before Carlos shouted at his colleague to stop before the squad car struck the vehicle ahead,

As men do, whether or not it is correct, Carlos stole his own glance before coming to his senses to the task at hand. She still read a hint of blush in the officer's cheeks. It was good to be reminded of the attraction of her assets.

"Oye, mano!" Officer Velez said to the driving patrolman. *"Ver el camino. La chica hermosa ayudará más tarde,"* Keep on the track. The beautiful gal can help us later on.

Marisol felt better about Carlos Velez, which gave her a sense of ease when the ambulance took a different route from the cruiser.

The rest of the drive lacked excitement as the patrolman restrained himself to driving, Carlos scanned their surroundings for threats, and *la soldado* uncrossed her legs and twiddled her thumbs between nervous kneecaps. After an interminable ten minutes, the three found themselves at the Cuartel General, department house of the Puerto Rico state police in San Juan.

Carlos led Marisol willingly into the building as the patrolman opened doors for them. She was led to an interrogation room with the two men before an administrative assistant came through the door and tapped Carlos on the shoulder. He excused himself and asked the patrolman to watch over her.

Divided by a bullet-proof glass indoor window to an adjacent room, Marisol's attention stayed on Officer Carlos Velez while he answered a telephone and the patrolman offered her coffee. She requested Bustelo with cream and sugar before he called the assistant to go get it.

La soldado waited for more info before offering any. If nothing else, she'd be peacefully assertive. She figured her perspective of Agent de Salinas and the late Luis Fernando would help *el uniformado* get a team to take down the Shelling Polk *pendejo* she'd heard about.

Marisol found it strange and somehow rewarding to work with honorable men for a change. It was also unnerving. She wouldn't hesitate to revert to survival mode once again if it was what events on the ground called for.

* * *

On the other end of the phone calling a state police tip line, Carey greeted Carlos with an *hola,* soon reminding him to keep his reaction on the down-low before she introduced herself again as Ron's wife. A month or so earlier, she'd met him in her house and she figured she could trust him now that all hell had broken loose.

Ron had said Officer Velez was *una policía* who followed the right rules and did what was best for the community. She had asked to speak to him through the tip line. Lack of red tape was a good sign

"Buenas tardes, señora," Carlos said in a smooth baritone. *"Por favor, continúe, no necesariamente en español."* Speak English if it makes you more comfortable.

Sipping an espresso at a local cafe, dressed in bulging cargo shorts and a tank top, Carey relayed in hushed English what she'd found at the Community Library. She described her experience as a hostage under whom she figured was Russell Thurgood. She reported real estate records of Thurgood and publicly-available evidence hinting at malfeasance by him and *narco* associates.

She continued that, for the last few days, she had been able to liberate herself from nasty *pendejos* trying to keep her down. Carey had beaten up dirty cops, "borrowed" a squad car, a rental, a Toyota, and then a motorcycle to stay a step ahead of predators in her pursuit of justice. An audible groan from the good Officer Velez interrupted her stream of consciousness on affairs.

"Carey, did you beat up the two guys taking you from the Metropolitan Detention Center?" Carlos said in a hushed, quick-paced voice that hinted annoyance. "They were on my side. They were told to tell you they'd deliver you safely and you shouldn't worry."

Carey gave a chuckle that was a bit reserved if embarrassed. The phone was quiet for a few seconds before she answered.

"One thing you never say to a woman in hopes she'll stay calm is to reassure her she has nothing to worry about. I'm paranoid with people I haven't met. Can you blame me? Corporate assholes put a bead on me. I didn't injure anyone for life, at least I hope."

Carlos returned a chuckle, asking in Spanish for her to repeat Thurgood's info so he could double-check intel. An audible pencil scratch signaled he was putting the property, criminal, and eyewitness information from her to paper.

"What's going on your end, Carlos? You doing okay? I really

am sorry for beating up your guys."

"We should have known better," he said in a hushed voice "We should get help from a friend of a friend, *un chota,* a snitch. He's a guy who I can call, especially when it comes to harassing *gringos.* He and your husband had an interesting encounter. Your information can only help us take out these *pendejos.* They are holding a useful witness. I have news about your boys too. I'm hesitant to share, but I know I can't keep secrets from *una madre.*"

Carey affirmed and listened as Carlos informed her of Ron's quest to Fajardo with the help of a rogue FBI agent. Municipal police chatter had mentioned *un niño y una veija* in a trailer. She agreed with Ron's assessment that "mercenary assholes" wouldn't waste time with diplomacy to deal with liabilities.

"I'd better be on my way to Fajardo," Carey said. "Good luck with the *hijo'e puta* in the capital."

Carlos said to her in Spanish that he'd get more done, thanking her for her information. He'd put extralegal plans in motion and then take a step back until someone rang for the cops, allowing him plausible deniability. He deadpanned that Ron and she both owed him expense-paid nights full of *cervesa y mujerzuelas* for skirting the law, so they ought to stay alive to pay him back.

"*Lo que, cabrón, buena suerte,*" Carey said. She didn't care about his need for booze and babes but wished him good luck.

Carey disconnected the call and finished her espresso. After bussing her table, she retraced her way back to the still untouched Suzuki. She started eastward with the bike after the sun had begun to disappear beyond the western horizon.

The pleasant, tropical air of spring typically lulled her to a sense of peace as her *moto* went just over the limit to Fajardo.

She prepared for the worst, wanting safety for her child and her husband. With all other events lost to the wind, Carey primed herself to do whatever was necessary

"Dios te salve, Maria. Llena eres de gracia..." Carey whispered the Ave Maria to herself. The words gave her strength as she raced into the unknown.

26

Hit the Fan

Ron didn't expect to his first view of Fajardo to be the rising of smoke from fiery debris where Margarita's trailer had been. A squad car with *dos policía municipal* and a Hummer filled with four well-armed tough guys was out of place as well.

The cops were likely waiting for fire investigators. The Hummer passengers identified themselves with authorities before scanning the perimeter. If not on the same payroll, Ron suspected both parties were getting kickbacks courtesy of Shelling-Polk. Ron considered them all hostiles.

The cops and the thugs occupied a space about one hundred feet from the fireball. Ron and Lopez took in the scene a good fifty feet west of them. Ron took out a Samsung burner from Carlos and dialed the number Margarita had given for emergencies. After about five seconds of listening to the receiver ring, a pebble hit Ron's left shoulder.

Ron turned left, aiming his pistol with the other hand. Surprised, but happy at what he saw, he pointed the Desert Eagle at once toward the ground before returning a grin.

Margarita stood near the base of a palm tree, holding John's hand in her right. His son's index finger dropped from a shushing gesture to reveal a cocky smirk. The Remington Pump Action was crooked in her left arm, pointed toward the ground.

Ron gave a look to Lopez that everything was okay before crouching to the ground and waving John over. The boy hurried over and let himself be embraced in his father's arms. After brief introductions, Ron asked Lopez to take his son and the boy's caretaker to the Honda CBRs. The cycles had been parked a short distance away. The primary mission was to keep innocents safe; the secondary was to see if Ron could get a glimpse of what was going on.

The guns for hire had smug looks Ron wished to wipe off. As they had a variety of high-powered firearms, Ron reminded himself he had to take events one step at a time. The cops stared dumbly at the burning trailer, sidearms holstered. He soon received a vibration signaling a call on the Samsung.

"Speak," Ron commanded with the efficiency of Hunter S. Thompson's ashes being shot out of a cannon.

"Your wife called. She's on her way out to Fajardo to protect her boys," Carlos replied. "*Qué pasa?*"

"There's a few *pendejos* here who've checked in with *la policía*. My son and his caretaker are doing well, thank goodness. Lopez is taking them to safety while I keep a lookout. You up to anything?"

"The state police are slow but safe. I'm calling in a favor from a *campesino* you confirmed as having an M2 Browning. *La chica,* Marisol, seems nice enough. You sure she shot at you with an automatic? I'd hate to charge her for possession of an illegal firearm. I'll turn a blind eye while she does her thing."

"Looked like Lopez's got a thing for her," Ron replied. "Play it safe and don't get hooked on the help. She's a real killer."

"I ain't looking for beef with *la chica* or our FBI pal," Carlos replied. "I just need help rescuing the *mujer* taken hostage from La Perla. I have my sights set on Russell Thurgood."

"At least my boy's safe," Ron replied. "I'll keep an eye out for my wife. Keep things tight on your end–"

Before signing off, an explosion erupted from where any remnants from the trailer had been. The blast knocked the Samsung from Ron's hand, and he hit the ground and shielded his eyes. He took in bits of light while trying to make sense of the nearby fire.

The whine of a Suzuki echoing along the PR-3 cut through any noise. The confusion was compounded with the blast of a shotgun from Margarita, a fairly far off burst of ignited magnesium from M84 stun grenades, and the whir of gunshots. Chaos rebounded from all sides.

Ron considered himself lucky to have shielded his eyes: he was still able to see well enough. Even though the M84 had detonated far enough away from him, phantom rings and spots hindered his coordination amid the pandemonium. He squinted and breathed as he saw that the two police had hit the deck.

The assholes from the Hummer soon exchanged fire with Margarita, who had separated from John and Lopez. She took cover behind a small, rusting 1980s Ford pickup, volleying fire with automatic pistols and an AR-15. *Los dos policía* were either smart or cowardly enough to continue to lie low.

Happy to have the Desert Eagle, Ron positioned the pistol in his right hand, steadying the sights with his left and breathing out before squeezing off a shot. A .45 round aimed near the flash of the AR-15 muzzle resulted in a scream and the semi-automatic stopped. A second of relief was quickly broken when he became the primary target.

With automatic gunfire exchanging quick cadenced lead with Margarita and Ron, the unmistakable whir and hum of a Suzuki *moto* wheezed from nearby. Gusts of exhaust puffed to mix with the acrid scent of gun propellant. The motorcycle driver shot off a handgun to draw fire from the mercenaries.

Ron's realized that the Suzuki-driver drawing attention from their position was likely his wife. From the relatively short distance, he thought he could see strong, slender arms extending from a tank top. Ron resigned himself to join Margarita to focus on the task at hand as the Suzuki kept moving in arcs, slowing its speed.

Blasts from the Remington and the Desert Eagle soon took down two more of the mercenaries. The remaining one got off a lucky shot to hit the Suzuki rear tire after it had slowed for an evasive turn. Ron silenced him with his last shot as the Suzuki slid to a halt. Margarita and he rushed from opposite directions toward the motorcyclist.

At the site of the grounded Suzuki, Ron shouted for his son when he saw his wife. He assessed her wounds at once while she held onto consciousness.

Carey had a rapid pulse and was still breathing, with a broken arm twisted at the elbow. Her teeth clenched as he looked at ripped pants and nasty abrasions along most of her leg. Ron did an initial concussion check.

Ron gave a firm pinch to her right hand and then her right shoulder, happy to see her grimace at both sensations. The snap of his fingers in front of her eyes made her blink before the still-sharp pupils followed his hand from left to right, to her forehead and her chin. Her teeth flashed when she gave her head a slight turn, showing pain from whiplash.

Lopez and John soon joined them as Margarita rushed to the Ford pickup to hot-wire it to an idle and drive it to them. In rapid-fire Spanish, she told John not to worry and told Lopez and Ron that Carey would be taken to *un médico, una amiga, no hospital.* Margarita's glance reassured Ron that his wife would be in safe hands, and she opened the door to the bed before taking John's hand and leading him to ride shotgun.

From a crouch, using his legs, Ron hooked his arms underneath Carey's shoulders after both Lopez and he got her to a sitting position. Lopez lifted her legs underneath the knees on the count of three as Ron stood. They transferred her to the truck bed, with Ron relieved that her legs responded from the firm jerks. Ron kissed her on the neck underneath her ear, again pleased with the response of a flush of blood to her head

"I've got to head to San Juan to help criminals rescue a woman from a jackass,," Ron said, trying to be nonchalant despite the gravity of the situation. "I love you and John and I've got the feeling you're in good hands."

Ron made a plea to the FBI agent to look after her. All three nodded, another sign Carey would be all right. She pursed her lips, still squinting with pain.

Ron then jogged to the passenger side of the truck, kissed his son on the forehead, and told Margarita to take care of his family. He checked his son John's lap belt as his heartbeat raced in time.

"No hay problema," Margarita said before starting the truck to a westward destination.

In the distance, *la policía* outside the remains of Margarita's trailer were getting into their cars as bomb squad units arrived on the scene. All friendlies were prepped to be gone by the time investigators or the SWAT Team would show.

Ron commandeered one of the Honda CBR motorcycles in which he'd arrived. He headed west to San Juan. Thoughts of worry about his family competed with a sense of duty and loyalty to recently acquired allies.

He had to kick some ass. The adrenaline rush from the gunfire with the mercenaries combined with the slow burn for his family to help him focus. Thurgood had been testing fate for a while. Ron would help execute the end game.

27

Playing Dirty

Marisol walked east on Calle Norzagaray just after midnight to mid-rise condos around where Russell Thurgood stayed in the penthouse. The warm breeze off the Atlantic was likely providing post-spring break tourists to a sense of leisure, but she was wound tighter than a clock at a train station to hell. Her thoughts rebounded back to the tasks set forth by Officer Carlos Velez, *el uniformado*.

The honorable officer pointed her in the direction of forces loyal to the Shelling-Polk Corporation at an address nearby to where she now stood. Earlier, after having dismissed the attending officer in the interrogation room, Carlos related what he knew to both her and a man listening over a burner phone.

The three put what could be considered a plan in place before Carlos escorted her out of the station and gave her thirty bucks, ostensibly for supplies she would need. He directed her where to meet his *chota,* his informer, and told her to be good.

Marisol was happy with the intel the officer provided to possibly help the *mujer* and her dependents after they'd sheltered her. It was also good any help on her part aligned with a more natural need to kick ass. All the better if that ass had pale skin and dreams of imperialism.

With the thirty bucks, she'd made a pit stop at La Plaza Las Américas to pick up a black T-shirt, a set of black cargo pants to replace her skirt, and a stuffed *tripleta* from a nearby food truck. After having finished the sandwich of pork, plantains, and cheese, she relieved herself and changed in a public restroom. With a freshly-scrubbed face and a stroll north, she waited outside the target luxury, mid-rise condo complex.

Near the same place where she'd slit Luis's throat, she was firing herself up to do what was necessary. She had to sneak in on some *hijos'e puta*, take them down, and be out when Officer Carlos Velez's official cavalry showed up.

The good Officer Velez was to then run an investigation. The results would lead the press to believe local criminals had ravaged Thurgood's office after a tip-off from *policía municipal* who felt they were shorted on deals with dirty US mainland interests. The official message wouldn't veer too far from the truth.

In an alley about fifty feet from where she stood, she noticed her contact behind a bin that shielded him from passersby. The 6-foot tall Willy Ortiz wore a pink *guayabera* that bulged over muscle underneath. He was said to be not well-known for subtlety.

When the two made eye contact, the *campesino* and *chota* opened the outer shirt to show he was dressed similarly to her. She approached with hands visible to her sides as he crouched to the ground.

"Estás bregando Chicky Starr?" Willy asked, in reference to the Puerto Rican professional wrestler. Marisol responded

the with two nods and a smirk as a security gesture. It was an agreement to fight dirty, if necessary.

After cordial-enough introductions, he crouched to open a black duffel bag and brought out two guns and extra magazines. He stood before handing her a matching Heckler & Koch MP5 automatic submachine gun equipped with a suppressor.

She took it before noticing the pair of M84 stun grenades on his vest above a set of M67 fragment grenades. He handed her an extra magazine he'd taken from the bag. She checked her MP5 and readied it.

For all the Rambo-style antics, she figured she held as many cards as the gun-for-hire. Willy and she exchanged intel off Norzagaray, watching the condo for weaknesses she could exploit.

The entryway showed a doorman with a walkie talkie and a shoulder-holstered pistol visible enough through the rack-bought suit. From the small distance, he appeared as bored and listless as a Walmart associate, moving behind a counter with a gaze surveying the lit patio leading to the building.

The relative subtlety was no doubt meant to downplay more advanced security procedures and firepower guarding the inside of the mid-rise structure. It couldn't be that easy to attack a crony corporate raider suckling subsidies from Uncle Sam. Could it?

Willy and she agreed against going balls to the wall in order to play events more coyly. She tied her T-shirt above her navel, pulling it tight across her braless, athletic breasts. The cuffs of her pants were rolled up past muscular calves to appear more flirty, like capris.

Marisol handed the prepped MP5 to Willy for him to hold in exchange for one of his M84s and asked for the pink shirt.

The *guayabera* was then wrapped around the flashbang, in a bundle in her left arm. She advanced off or Norzagaray with a sway to her hips.

The doorman flunky met her at the top of a number of stairs. He asked her to stop and state her business. He looked nervous or bashful all of a sudden.

She gave a giggle that sounded as natural as that of a college cheerleader. That, and a look that more fit the part of fun-seeking coed rather than skilled soldier seemed to work magic. In a higher-pitched voice than usual, she responded she was here to help with recreation for the man in charge.

The doorman was gearing for the bait. A flash of rouge hinted his olive-toned cheeks as his eyes grew less focused, glancing at her abs. She hooked him with a cadenced flex of her leg beneath the right knee.

"*Perdóname, señorita*," the doorman said, averting his eyes before speaking into his walkie talkie. He told the receiver, security presumably, that a *chica* was looking to party with *el jefe*. A voice on the other end responded to frisk her and send her to *el ático*. The penthouse was the target.

"*Tienes un cigarro, señor?*" she asked before he could frisk her, pursing her lips with her best Rosario Dawson impression. She added that she needed him to rescue her with the smoke before she got to work. She got off a little after one.

The man took her to his counter before setting down the walkie talkie. She waited, swaying her hips while he fished in his pockets for a cigarette and a lighter. She posed no threats while accepting the cigarette and leaning forward for a flame.

When he leaned in to set the cigarette alight, she struck him across the Adam's apple with a lightning-quick chop with her left. The blow wasn't hard enough to kill, but it did incapacitate the first notch in the building's security.

She crouched to the ground as he fell, not quick enough to slow his descent, but enough to blow him a kiss before delivering a smack to the temple. She took his security card for access to the elevator.

Marisol nodded in the distance for Willy to advance. She held the flashbang in her right hand, giving a slight wave with the other using the *guayabera.*

The six-foot-tall, mahogany-skinned *campesino* joined her side at once. His terse lips were curved at the ends with a *mierda*-eating grin. After a chuckle, he handed Marisol the fully prepped MP5, handle toward her.

La soldado, Marisol, could have sworn the beefy ruffian was attempting to flirt. His lively eyes peered down at her, glancing down her body. She put that presumption to rest by feigning a kick to the unconscious guard's groin, then meeting Willy's eyes

"*Preguntas, hijo'e puta?*" Marisol said. Questions, son of a bitch?

"*No, señorita.*" Willy said with a shrug, averting her scowl.

He mumbled that he was of the school to never hit a woman, even if she threatened your *machismo.* No one wanted to mess with those kinds of *mujeres.* He held his hand out, without an iota of threat, waiting for instruction.

Marisol decided that *el chota, el campesino* had at least been raised right.

"*Vámonos,*" she said, gesturing toward the elevator.

She continued in a whisper that they ought to expect fresh hell. So that's what they prepared for as they ascended to the top floor penthouse. She returned the MP5 to Willy in exchange for the other flashbang, hiding it in the *guayabera.*

The flashy shirt was then wrapped to settle around her hips.

Marisol figured an attack from the elevator would be more of a surprise as a direct route. She gave the plan to Willy that she'd provide a distraction and a flare up before he attacked with his MP5. The automatic, access to grenades, and the way she'd use her own natural assets was more than enough to make her cocky.

The appearance of a good time girl was expected, per security confirmation. Marisol could play the part but had methods and a reason to kill.

* * *

Russell Thurgood expected either a call girl, exotic food delivery, or both when the chime for the elevator sounded in his penthouse. He'd found the best Chinese east of Austin on the island and had worked out after hours delivery of food and girls in exchange for opiates, some of which were legal with a prescription. He was high on his own medication as the elevator opened, his mouth watering.

A young gal, who appeared slightly too skinny than was his preference, pranced through the entrance. Her sporty look and hint of shyness, along with the sway of her hips was enough to overlook any perceived imperfection. He put his hands over his paunch and called his guards to relax precautions as he lulled himself to false security.

No one else was visible from outside the elevator. The drugstore cowboy-in-charge motioned for two of four guards in the penthouse to check the gal out. Better them than him to meet a surprise. He wasn't that dumb. No alarm bells rang in his brain at the moment, but he erred on the side of caution while in foreign lands.

Thurgood figured there might be repercussions from any action in Fajardo and La Perla, but figured a fit gal in capris would only raise his heart rate in a good way. He still kept Jimmy Ocasio on speed dial, having yet to press a button for his narco-connected security head to check in.

Ocasio only had to travel via stairs one floor up. He was otherwise busy leading three guards to watch a room where Adderall-fueled accountants laundered money. Thurgood was more concerned about losing a large supply of prescription-protected amphetamines than the loss of any manpower. Either way, he thought it wise to protect business capital.

The four guards in Thurgood's penthouse were bald headed *Boricuas* who'd worked for Luis Fernando. They surrounded the boss in a square formation, cocking Beretta 93R automatics with three round bursts selected.

The two who'd advanced to meet the *chica* looked professional enough, if not expecting a fight. The two others turned from their window stations to focus protection on the *gringo* guaranteeing their paychecks. As with any routine security job, none of the four looked to relax while the boss got his rocks off.

The two tasked with another pat-down stopped a couple yards from the elevator. A mahogany-skinned forearm flashed from an elevator blind spot and didn't linger for anyone's aim, only agitating to disrupt the periphery of the guards' view.

A four-letter-word slipped from Thurgood's mouth after the *chica* shook her waist, dropping what looked like two compact Maglites to the ground. They clinked on dark marble tile, and she silently fell soon after. Before any guards could react, she retreated toward the elevator with a backward roll to mimic the best jiu-jitsu-trained stunt double.

The M84 grenades soon threw forth a set of thunderous booms and two flashes of over one million candelas of ignited magnesium. The stun knocked the two forward guards to the ground before the other two returned 9mm Parabellum rounds.

With the Berettas' magazines eventually in need of changing, a mahogany-skinned man slightly showed from the elevator. With a firm handle on an MP5, *el negro* efficiently aimed to take out the guards in front. He and the *chica* took a split second to resume cover in blind spots.

Thurgood let out a little urine after he hit the deck. At the end of another round of fire from his remaining two guards' Berettas, the duo in black from the elevator returned automatic 9mm fire. The caramel-skinned girl combatant also had an MP5. The drugstore cowboy let out a few choice words before emptying a bit more of his bladder. He'd had enough sense to speed dial Ocasio to ascend to action from the floor below.

One of the Thurgood's guards showed more competent than the average drug enforcer. The bald *Boricua* with a tattooed face had ducked at the ricocheting rounds of MP5 sub-machine guns. He calmed himself, inhaling and exhaling while reloading, slowing down time in his mind to focus aim on a speck of mahogany skin.

Parabellum rounds from tattoo face's Beretta soon hit one of the intruders, initiating a growled baritone *"coño"* from the elevator. The tide turned further when Thurgood, the *gringo-in-charge* found his urine-splattered *cojones* and located the Ruger .357 Magnum he'd recently purchased on the black market.

Using the firearm training he'd received from dirty cops,

he and his remaining useful guard put the intruders on the defensive. The other *Boricua* guard shot his Beretta toward the elevator without any accuracy.

Only one MP5 returned well-aimed, better-timed fire.

Thurgood and tattoo face made like the Bolivians in *Butch Cassidy and the Sundance Kid.* Usually more a smarmy politician than an operator, the Shelling-Polk shill longed to buttress his gunslinger pretension. He counted on Ocasio to clinch the win.

"This bitch is harder to put down than a pit bull in heat," he said, holding his position and his piss. Backup appeared to have been held up.

28

Rock the Penthouse

The mid-rise off of Calle Norzagaray was where Ron Riley was most needed. After examining the unconscious doorman in the lobby and subsequent unwillingness to rely on the elevator, he sighed when he saw the ten stories of stairwell above him. The previous events of the evening jolted him with adrenaline reserves to power him through.

Over a text, while riding west, Officer Carlos Velez had given Ron the address. He'd been told to expect state police to respond once locals reported a disturbance of the peace. Ron hadn't expected to meet any resistance on the ground floor, knowing from the text that the assassin wannabe, Marisol, was working with the kidnapper wannabe, Willy, to lay the groundwork for a raid. He had already relieved the doorman of a shoulder holstered Glock 17 semi-automatic 9mm after having ditched the empty Desert Eagle.

The rattling of automatic gunfire from above, some of which was suppressed, told him to hurry. No time like the present. He raced up the steps, interrupted by the click of military boots from above.

From the floor below the penthouse, Ron noticed two targets with heavy artillery ascending. He took a moment to shoot the Glock at the wall, hoping to draw attention without thinking through repercussions.

"Policía, hijo'e puta," Ron shouted, hoping, despite instinct, that the announcement of law enforcement would command respect. With many police corrupt or easily bought, his hopes for any authority were met with automatic gunfire. At least he was realistic enough to take cover toward the wall beforehand. He waited until the spurt of gunfire stopped.

Ron continued up the steps. He stayed to the periphery of the stairwell with the realization his cover was diminishing as he ascended. Whoever was holding the line below the penthouse had tossed an object down the shaft, fragmenting when it hit the ground floor.

He was safe enough from the blast to take a few breaths before charging forward. His stress was reaching Mosul levels, which wasn't good for anyone awaiting the bad end of his standard police-issue semi-automatic.

"These shitbags are going overkill," he said to himself after stifling his desire to shout.

Ron wanted to shoot a couple 9mm rounds but figured he'd save ammo and release steam through the rest of his sprint up the steps. *Un pendejo* responded by dropping another explosive, missing again by a few floors.

Saving bullets for the fight above was a good choice. The clickety-clack of steps heading downward made Ron nervous until a couple of explosions from the penthouse rocked the supports above him. A few screams and final automatic bursts led to a muffled mess.

The man setting shady deals for Shelling-Polk was probably

in trouble. Ron reasoned Thurgood might already be dead or dying. The eerie quiet after the chaos allowed Ron to continue to the floor beneath the penthouse. The air was dusty as he peeked around a door frame, set to exit the stairwell.

His first task was shooting the indecisive bastard twenty feet away. The flunky had a Beretta automatic pistol, but not the wherewithal to either go to help the boss above or properly guard whoever was in a nearby suite.

Ron took a few seconds to aim and shoot, hitting the man's femur. Lack of blood spurts showed he'd missed the artery, which he took as good news. The shouts from within the suite and a latent exchange of automatic gunfire from above would've struck Ron harder if he'd allowed himself to think he was safe.

He put his back to the wall on the other side of the door frame leading to the suite and released a large breath. Whoever had screamed was in trouble. Ron grabbed the man he'd just shot to use as cover, a hostage, or bait. With the still-living shield, he covered himself except for the Glock 17, appearing in the entryway.

"*No te acerques más,*" said a gravelly voice. The macho message was clear: back off.

Ron responded, stepping back and pointing the Glock to his hostage's head. The sound of slow footsteps on the stairwell behind called him to make a quick move. He ordered in slow Spanish to let any hostages go.

The asshole in the suite made Ron's course of action easier by shooting Ron's hostage in the face. Ron had anticipated the splatter of blood and brain matter as much as the lack of honor among thugs.

In the split second that followed the doorway horror show,

Ron aimed his Glock toward the man opposite him and took the shot. The goon soon dropped an automatic pistol due to the hole in his head. The body followed.

Three unarmed clerks in business casual crouched and fidgeted like dope fiends clawing at imaginary spiders as Ron walked toward them with the Glock at his side. One was still shrieking.

Ron kept a respectful distance, which was easy enough because he wasn't in a comforting mood unless safe with his wife and son. The brain matter on his face didn't make him feel cuddly, either.

"*Calmarse, por favor. Puedo ayudarte,*" Ron replied after wiping his face with his forearm. Stay calm. I can help you.

To the three's credit, they quieted as Ron refocused his attention down the hall to the stairwell. He saw a familiar face he'd been told was friendly, contrary to their brief shared history. After evading gunfire, exploded craniums, and cranked-up hostages, he decided to try to relax based on what the FBI man, Lopez, had said about the woman who'd tried to kill him.

Marisol had shot a MAC-10 at him weeks ago but also seemed to have quite a bit of affection for Agent Roberto Lopez. That agent had been the same guy who'd abducted him near Fajardo, so the bar was set low for placement of trust.

At least she was pointing the MP5 in her hand toward the ground. He realized he didn't have much choice with allies as he waved her into the suite.

Marisol soon entered, placed the submachine gun on the floor, and approached the scared spectators. The three were attempting to calm themselves fiercely, despite whatever junk was jolting their systems. The soldier spoke in Spanish too rapid and soft for Ron to understand, but the results were what was needed as tensions cooled faster than spent brass. The sound of sirens from the state police from below somehow comforted Ron as the five started to leave the suite to make their way out of the mid-rise.

Ron was the only one armed, pointing the Glock to the floor with no finger in the trigger guard. Marisol led the captives with a gentle touch. Everything seemed alright as a few other residents on the floor joined them to get to the stairs.

Once through the doorway to the stairwell, a jab from the left knocked Ron's head to render him woozy. He dropped the Glock before *la soldado* started yelling with more anger than fear.

With the thought that Thurgood was dead or otherwise neutralized, his wife and his son safe enough, and help from friends was on the way, Ron let himself take the rest of the morning off. Again, it wasn't like he had much of a choice to the matter, so he might as well not worry.

A flood of fatigue washed over Ron, rushing him toward unconsciousness. En route, he felt his body lifted up, which might have worried Ron about a possible ascent to heaven if he wasn't expecting a trip in the opposite direction. A sense of his body descending put him oddly more at ease as feeling left him.

* * *

Willy Ortiz had pissed off Marisol almost enough for her to smack him with the butt of her MP5 if she had been still carrying it. At one time, she'd been ordered to kill the *gringo*, Ron Riley, and now it was her task to protect him. Willy's knocking him out seemed an unnecessary barrier to escape.

Willy only returned a smile and raised a finger to his lips at her yelling. He had toughed out the grazing gun wound, having wrapped it with duct tape before joining her to escape down the stairwell with his bag of goodies. The crafty *campesino* soon showed that she'd underestimated him.

In his duffel bag, the tall, mahogany-skinned, left-wing, gun-loving farmer took out navy blue button-downs resembling those of emergency medical technicians with the Cuerpo de Emergencias Médicas de Puerto Rico.

Marisol sighed before they changed costume to make the exit smoother, even with an unconscious *gringo*. Leaving behind the two MP5s seemed more painful, but necessary if any authorities who weren't Officer Carlos Velez decided to pay them attention.

Willy hoisted the *gringo* on an uninjured shoulder as she snatched the fallen Glock 17 on a whim. She tucked it in her back waistband, reasoning it blended in under the button-down of her disguise. The emptied duffel bag and pink *guayabera* awaited on the floor beneath the penthouse for investigators to puzzle over.

The three strung out *pendejo*s in business casual followed passively as Marisol led the way. The *campesino* and the *gringo* brought up the tail end. Descending the stairs, they stayed close to the walls for any support. The escape was peaceful enough until the final flight to the ground floor.

Marisol heard a grunt from behind her like the one Willy had given when automatic gunfire had hit him in the penthouse elevator. Two thumps hit the ground as sandbags set to weigh down a carnival tent.

The three stragglers had made an escape by the time she'd

turned around and pulled the Glock semi-automatic from her waistband. She was sick and tired of this shit. A familiar *cabrón* was in her sights.

The late Luis Fernando's security head had punched Willy in the wound and now aimed his Beretta automatic with shaky hands from twenty feet away. If he wanted to kill her, he had his chance now at close range. The Glock in Marisol's hands could take him down just as surely.

As state law enforcement locked down the lobby beyond the next door, the two with guns returned glances before the man gave a nod of recognition. Any prolonged stand-off would be a waste of time. Marisol told him so, remembering his name, Jimmy Ocasio.

Ocasio had weaseled his way to two high-paying jobs, she explained to him, surviving the death of two bosses while keeping his reputation.

La soldado asked if the putz wanted to throw all that away by dying for his honor. Both pistols were cocked and ready to go. Marisol told him it was his choice, but she didn't feel like dying today. Also, she couldn't eliminate every asshole, even if she wanted to.

Willy stayed on the ground throughout the back and forth, making his way slowly to take advantage. It turned out he wasn't subtle enough. Ocasio knocked him out with a kick to the temple before he lowered his gun.

Marisol mimicked the disarmament, keeping her finger over the trigger guard until her counterpart released his magazine and emptied the chamber. She followed suit, and they returned a resigned nod.

Ocasio went up the stairs, probably to look for a service exit. Marisol left Willy and the *gringo* on the ground where they'd be safe, for the moment. She wiped prints off of the Glock, laid on the ground, and appeared in the lobby, palms visible.

In her navy blue button-down, she blended in enough with emergency medical technicians monitoring the still-unconscious desk guard and civilians going through shock. She made a beeline toward Officer Carlos Velez and addressed him directly rather than wait for questions.

Marisol told Officer Velez she had to defend herself against aggression in the penthouse, adding that Willy and the *gringo* were recovering beyond the lobby at the base of the stairwell. The men would recover, she responded, adding with a look of worry that they hadn't found the *mujer* missing from the shootout in La Perla.

"*Ella está a salvo. La encontramos. Buen trabajo, señorita. Si puedo ayudarle con algo más?*" Officer Carlos Velez said after Marisol was done. The woman is safe. We found her. Good work, miss. May I help you with something else?

Marisol managed a smile before nodding and saying she was feeling fine. The brevity was welcome. She left from where she'd sashayed in within the past hour. She had to admit it was fulfilling to use her special skills for some good.

La mujer y dos niños were okay. In time, she planned to reconnect with another *hombre de honor* whom she had met the past week.

29

The Locals

Just before dawn, Agent Roberto Lopez handed another joint to Dr. Maria Perez. The pretty, thirtysomething veterinarian and he were relaxing in one of the shacks of Equine Hacienda, a horse farm about twenty minutes west of Fajardo. They chuckled as he nodded to his cast-aside FBI credentials.

Lopez, Carey, John, and Margarita had arrived at the farm after the shootout, with Margarita and the boy taking immediate shelter in lodge accommodations on the grounds. Before the first hour of the morning, Dr. Perez had fixed Carey up on a sterile-as-could-be cot, promptly injected her with a human dose of Ketamine, sterilized the leg wound with iodine, and set the arm before applying ice and gauze where needed.

Up until the present, the good doctor and he were keeping wounds clean. They made the decision to smoke a joint with Carey to help with any stress from tedium. Dr. Perez recommended cannabis as a less dangerous way to manage pain, inflammation, and ensure recovery. Agent Lopez agreed with the doctor's plan of action.

A knock at the door jolted them through the haze.

"How's Mama," John said on the opposite side. Dr. Perez tended to the patient as Agent Lopez opened the door, waving away smoke and faking a cough.

"Some hay caught fire, but it's out, and *tu madre* recovers, *hombrecito*," the Fed said.

Margarita accompanied the boy, with a look of solid granite on her face for the FBI agent and veterinarian, who was also her niece.

The hint of a grin appeared when Margarita and the boy saw a very stoned Carey. With bloodshot, wandering eyes and no signs of pain, Carey beckoned her son and the caretaker to come inside. Mama Riley's mouth was full of cotton and smiles.

"*Se lo ganó*," Margarita said, chuckling. She's earned it.

After signalling all present to snuff out the smokes, the eldest woman motioned for John to join his mother before entering the shack herself.

The veterinarian and the FBI agent waved the fumes from the small space within. Dr. Perez set a glass of water to her patient's side before stepping outside with Lopez. Smiles erupted all around, despite some jangled nerves.

Between the potential, if unlikely snitch and Margarita, whom she called *tía*, Dr. Perez appeared she couldn't relax. The *ganja* paranoia didn't help, but she gave a healthy sigh when Lopez clapped her on the shoulder and gave a *mierda-*eating grin.

Lopez shrugged and handed her a snuffed-out joint before telling her to relax. After going to relieve himself in some bushes, a Samsung flip phone Carlos had given him buzzed. He answered with his free hand.

"*Qué tal, cabrón?*" he asked into the receiver,

Lopez listened, nodding with an occasional, *"Sí, mano."*

After clicking the phone shut, rearranging, and zipping his fly, the FBI man returned to Dr. Perez and excused himself from the situation at hand to attend to official business. Their host nodded when Lopez assured no law enforcement eyes on cannabis use. He went to the shack to bid his fellow guests *adios*.

Lopez told Margarita and Carey he had to head to San Juan. He would meet with Officer Carlos Velez and an agent from the mainland to clear the air and set any conclusions in the right direction. When Carey asked about which agent was sent from the mainland, his answer seemed to put her at ease.

"Agent Matt Russo. A friend of Ron, *sí?*" Lopez said. "He just landed from Miami."

"Sí. Todo bien, " Carey responded before smiling through the lingering haze.

Lopez and Dr. Perez left and went to the 1980s Ford pickup in which he had arrived earlier in the morning with *los mujeres y el niño.* The holes from gun blasts were sure to hinder his attempts to reenter society, so he asked the good doctor if she could lend a ride. He was going to keep the authorities off her back, after all.

Dr. Perez opened up nearby garage by hand, ushering him inside. Along with fertilizer and a cabinet she proclaimed was natural medicine for the horses, Lopez saw a street legal Suzuki DR dirt bike. She offered to lend it to him along with a bag to hold his gun and other goodies. She also gave him a helmet.

Agent Lopez thanked her, checked his Glock compact, and told her to expect the bike in a week or so. The Suzuki's motor whined when he accelerated from the farm. The ride only allowed him to feel more at ease when he hit smooth asphalt of the PR-66 west.

A little more than a half hour later, Lopez was able to get a brief shower and a change of clothes in the locker room at the San Juan FBI field office. A cup of Bustelo helped wake him before his meeting with Officer Carlos Velez and Agent Russo. It was about an hour before noon.

The Fed opposite him, dressed conservatively in an off-the-rack suit, had the physique of a drill sergeant. Supervisory Special Agent Matt Russo stood as Lopez offered a hand. The grip was as tightly-chiseled as the ebony crew cut on Russo's head.

Lopez was running on fumes. The lack of sleep and the remnants of cannabis-induced fatigue were overtaking any rush from adrenaline and caffeine. He was still unsure about which outcome he was staring in the face. Would it be prison time or a promotion?

Carlos Velez broke the professional tension, twisting the few hairs of his ebony mustache before giving his report in English on the attack where Shelling-Polk Corporation's representative in Puerto Rico had been staying. The fallout between dirty police, local criminals, and US mainland corporate interests had left Russell Thurgood deceased, he reported.

Initial reports suggested the cause of death was due to explosions and automatic weapons fire between guards loyal to Thurgood and criminals in the mid-rise off Calle Norzagaray. There were seven men found dead along with Thurgood in the state police sweep of the penthouse and the floor below.

"An FBI task force has been investigating collusion between police and grifters, drug dealers, and other criminals in Puerto Rico," Russo added, directing the news to Lopez. "My local source on the island, who you've met, alerted me of events, and later contacted Officer Velez to follow up. I've checked in with local federal agents and would appreciate your candor. I understand there might be trouble in the ranks of the FBI. I only volunteered to advise and assist local FBI with events based on info reported to me."

Lopez released a scant sigh to show some relief before Russo offered a cigarette.

He took a seat before accepting a Lucky Strike and a light. Russo's wry grin showed he didn't care as much about the rules as much as whether *pendejos* got what was coming. Lopez felt the approach was best at keeping with the original intent of the law, which put both he and Russo on good terms.

"Agent Russo," Lopez said. "I've been following corruption and criminal elements for a little over a week in the field. I saw some crazy stuff. How can I help with the investigation?"

"You can start with your recollection of events after having come into contact with my source on the ground here, Ron Riley," the drill sergeant agent said before giving a subtle nod. "I understand some of the details may be muddied, given your circumstance. I should remind you that I'm only collecting information to serve an advisory function."

Lopez never mentioned Marisol, and kept testimony vague enough so no one needed to press further about her. Officer Carlos Velez knew better than to interrupt with details about La Perla, *la soldado,* or *la mujer y dos niño*s who were caught in the crossfire.

Russell Thurgood, Luis Fernando, well-armed paramilitary thugs, and corruption dominated the truth-telling, with focus drawn from helpless actors, sexy soldiers, and horse farmers west of Fajardo. Assistant Special-in-Charge Agent Rodriguo de Salinas struck him as a shady character, and he relayed those suspicions.

After the statement, Agent Lopez shook hands with Agent Russo and then Officer Velez. No longer under scrutiny, Lopez took *el uniformado* aside and informed him where Ron and he would be able to find Carey and John. He then returned the good officer's Glock 26.

Carlos Velez said he'd call a cab to have Carey and her boy transported to the Hospital San Francisco and then get in touch with Ron. The two shook hands.

After leaving the San Juan field office, Lopez returned to his borrowed Suzuki and set off for his one-bedroom apartment in Miramar to get some sleep. He'd been away from his bachelor pad for over a week, and he missed the relative comforts of his bed and shower.

He planned to make a check-in with the office and ask further about his future with the FBI after twelve hours of unconsciousness. He hoped to find a way to reconnect with Marisol at some point.

After a shower and a meal of eggs, cheese, and beans sprinkled with chili powder, he watched cartoons to relax. He found a joint in the goody bag Dr. Perez had handed him earlier in the day. The cannabis helped him wind down before shucking his clothes in the bedroom. Sleep came easy.

30

Law and Order

Agent Matt Russo felt the rush of important work while liaising intel with a new local source in San Juan. He'd explained to Agent Lopez that he'd pass on the statement about his observations to the Miami Public Corruption Task Force.

Lopez seemed more relaxed after giving his statement, noting afterward that he expected to be kept in the loop with events on the ground. Russo figured he would advocate for Lopez. The agent had, against all odds and reason, been a stand-up guy for Ron and would be a capable go-to guy for future coordination on the island.

The Miami task force would work well with Agent Lopez in San Juan. In its first year, the operation was already coming under the label "Guard Shack." Russo was pleased to not get too involved in local politics. Better to pass the buck after the initial investigation. As a volunteer liaison, his primary interest was arranging for the Rileys to come back stateside. Any further investigations might make him tattle on the good guys. That was a job for higher-ups and HR departments.

Since Officer Carlos Velez had introduced himself as a friend of Ron's a few hours before getting Lopez's statement, Russo presumed he could be more candid with *el uniformado*. The officer showed he was game throughout, even leading Russo for lunch at the nearby Cayo Caribe.

Officer Velez ordered two shots of *ron anejo,* with a Miller Lite chaser before they could look at a menu. Carlos explained he could call an end to his shift after being on the job for more than twenty-four hours. He didn't give a *mierda* while he was off the clock, so he asked Agent Russo to not to be a wuss and give it to him straight.

Agent Russo ordered an iced tea and gave a smile.

"*Tacos de pescado?*" he asked before receiving a nod from Officer Velez and ordering in his limited Spanish. He offered *el uniformado* a cigarette, soon being met with a stern look and a smack to the hand.

"With some laws, I don't care, even in government offices," Carlos Velez said. "But the owners don't like smoke. *Su abuela* died of cancer, so if you flame up in here, I'll arrest you; I don't give a damn who you are. By the way, thanks for paying, *gringo.*"

Russo gave a smile such as he usually saved for his wife, his daughter, and his few genuine friends. He put away the Lucky Strikes and sipped his iced tea.

"So tell me your side of events from this morning," Russo said. "Ron vouches for you. I want to help set up events as best as they can before bringing Ron, Carey, and their son stateside. What really happened to Thurgood and anyone guarding the mid-rise on Calle Norzagaray? Why'd you go there in the first place?"

Carlos chuckled before downing the second shot.

"I've been forced to trust people," *el uniformado* said. "Like

Ron said, you're trying to kick the sauce and your act backs it up. It is a good reason to think you're someone I can trust, off the record."

Agent Russo sipped his iced tea and smirked. Carlos nodded his head toward his beer as the fish tacos arrived, returning an easy smile no doubt made more natural by fine rum.

"I sent *una soldado y un chota,* a soldier and a snitch, to check on Thurgood's condo, thinking the *pendejo* was holding *una mujer,* a woman, missing from an earlier *salpafuera* in La Perla. I assume any harm to Thurgood resulted from my contacts' self-defense. As you say in the US, it was a real clusterf-"

"Thanks, I've heard the term *salpafuera,*" Russo interrupted. "So what about this *mujer*, the soldier, and your snitch.

"*Los uniformados* had already recovered *la mujer* for safe-keeping, and she'll get back together with *los niños* in due time," Carlos continued. "*La soldado* and el *chota* helped out and parted ways after the action. You have a lot of good people on the mainland just looking to help out, *sí?*"

"*Entiendo*, Officer Velez," Russo said. "I understand I shouldn't be worried. Do you have anything to add about Fernando or any other *narcos?*"

Carlos took a bite of his lunch and sipped his beer. He cleared his throat before the bartender served him water.

"Slightly more than what you can read in the papers," he replied after a minute. "With Luis Fernando, I'd say the *pendejo* got what was coming to him. A routine investigation only showed a scared hooker and a few stray hands. A few associates of Luis showed up dead the last couple days and this morning, including seven around Thurgood's penthouse. I have a feeling we didn't account for all *los gamberros.*"

Russo gave a sigh before finishing his tea. Carlos continued, giving candid cooperation.

"I don't think you give a damn what happens here, as long as Ron stays out of the press and the killers and thieves bothering him and his family are dealt with," Carlos said. "I'll give your guy in Miami any intel I have to help him make a case. We know better than to make Uncle Sam look bad. *Entiendes?*

The cop and the Fed exchanged nods and finished lunch, peppered with occasional inane banter over the real definitions of football and soccer. Officer Carlos Velez's only serious comment was that he hoped to make sergeant soon. After barely following a match on the TV, *el uniformado* almost fell asleep in a dish of guacamole. Russo patted him on the back just in time, ordering water for the man.

With a vague memory of Ron having done the same for him, Russo ordered a cab and walked Carlos to it. He gave the driver more than enough to deliver the state policeman to his rental in Carolina.

Russo then got in his rented Camry, stopped at a drugstore to pick up a box of Nicorette, and made his way back to the field office. After checking in with Miami and local FBI, he filed the necessary paperwork and wrote commendations for Lopez and Velez.

Agent Russo made plans to visit Carey and Ron at the hospital in a day or so. He planned to then put forth the offer he had finagled from his superiors. Ron might be less loathe to work with the FBI if it could help him with WITSEC, make a more comfortable life for John and the wife, and allow a more regular routine back stateside.

But then again, Russo figured the "wanna-be jarhead" would have to make up his own damn mind on whether to accept help from a friend. As the saying goes, one can only bring a horse to water.

He then drove his rental to the Sheraton to settle in and call his wife and daughter. In the king suite, which was much better than the hourly room in Little Haiti's Saturn Hotel, Russo fired up his Toshiba and cracked an O'Doul's.

Zoe and Clara's faces soon appeared over Skype, and all the rigidity in his cheekbones relaxed under a still well-coiffed crew cut. His daughter started out blowing a kiss before they started the bedtime routine with a story. The sign off with his wife ended with lascivious laughter to keep him longing,

Russo popped a Nicorette and another O'Doul's as he sat on the small balcony off his room. From the Sheraton, a sense of serenity set amid lights glimmering around the San Juan skyline.

31

Recovery

"*Bendita tú eres entre todas las mujeres. Y bendito es el fruto de tu vientre,*" said the voice at Carey's side. Blessed are you among women. And blessed is the fruit of your womb.

After her eyes opened, she saw a middle-aged nun saying the beautiful words. As her vision focused, the sister continued, running strong fingers over rosary beads attached to her neck. The nun's other hand rested on Carey's forehead.

Carey blushed and smiled, muttering *gracias* after the sister quenched her thirst with water from a hospital mug. The blessings rendered her calm.

Words still escaped Carey as a morphine drip made the world cloudy. She vaguely remembered an official-looking Latino, Margarita, her son, horses, the smell of cannabis, and a kind Latina cleaning her wounds. She recalled the numbing, warm sensation of being high, which she only remembered from years ago before she had learned she was pregnant with John. Dull aches in her arm and leg softly smoldered as she said thank you again to the nun, and attempted a smile of gratitude.

"*Dónde estamos, sor?*" Carey managed. Where are we, sister?

"Hospital San Fransisco," the sister responded and went to the door of the room, calling to someone outside.

Carey worried for a moment, unsure of what to expect given the surprises of the past weeks. Attempts to prepare for self-defense were unnecessary. Her fists relaxed and her smile bloomed as a familiar face came in the room. The nun stayed, acting as a calming presence.

"*Buenas días, Señora* Carey," Agent Matt Russo said with a cordial grin. "I see you are recovering and in good hands. Your husband and son are safe for now."

"Hell, Matt," she managed with a voice hindered by dryness before the good sister gave her another drink of water. "It's good to see you. How'd you get to our corner of the world?"

Russo politely asked the nun to leave for a moment before he got to brass tacks. After a nod of approval from Carey, Ron's FBI friend and she were left alone.

His trip to the island came after her husband called for help to fight against threats from shady characters. Russo and Ron's work helped connect the dots for an ongoing FBI task force into corruption between crony capitalists, crooked cops, and criminals. More media attention with the explosive death of Shelling-Polk executive, Russell Thurgood, was something desk jockeys and politicians wanted to avoid.

Carey flinched with the mention of the man who'd taken her hostage. Russo gave her a nod, putting a soft hand on her shoulder after drawing closer.

Russo said he had pointed out to Miami superiors the faults of the family's protection and handling by FBI brass in Puerto Rico, getting concessions and some relocation money. Russo offered Ron protection and plausible deniability in exchange for cooperation as a private investigator in an anonymous suburb near Miami. He and Ron wanted to check with the boss, first, he said, nodding to Carey.

To push her own perspective on the matter, Carey told Russo to again bring in the nun to pray with her. He did so and waited quietly as they started.

"Padre nuestro que estás en los cielos, santificado sea tu nombre...," they said. Our father who art in heaven, hallowed be thy name...

Carey was ready for a return to normalcy, whatever that meant. Life as a fugitive in a US commonwealth had proven difficult, despite all the benefits of local culture and climate. She decided to allow the agreement formed by Ron and Matt Russo. She would need to first say goodbye to Margarita, her fellas at the gun range, and make sure other affairs were in order.

"Y no nos metas en tentación, mas líbranos de mal," the nun said, leading an end to the prayer. And lead us not into temptation, but deliver us from evil.

Carey then made her demands known, while agreeing to the new reality.

"Carey," Russo said. "I'll see to it that you get what's required. Ron told me he's in the first steps of arranging low-key goodbyes. We've been in touch with Margarita. Does that work for you?

"Bien," Carey replied.

"Do you want to see your husband and son now?" Russo asked.

She raised her fist and asked what took the agent so long.

Seconds after Russo gave the okay down the hall, John came running in. The boy gently rested his head on her side. Ron came in next, meandering toward her as if still recovering himself. He gave her a soft peck on the cheek.

"Hey, beautiful," Ron said. "You ready for a vacation? I made some colorful acquaintances around Caguas whom you may know. After goodbyes, we can make like tourists before returning to the mainland."

"Let's take it a step at a time," she said, smiling at her boys, Russo, and then toward the nun. "I'm surrounded by good people. That and my health are what I got going for me."

32

Despacito

Agent Lopez appeared in the scope's target hairs as he slowed the Suzuki dirt bike along the country road to Equine Hacienda, the horse farm outside Fajardo. He looked well-rested one week after having left the farm to meet Supervisory Special Agent Matt Russo and Officer Carlos Velez in San Juan.

Upon arrival at *la hacienda's* first shack, he swung his left leg over the rear wheel to disembark. A pretty woman, who looked like a hippie animal rights activist on her third master's degree, rushed to meet him, dressed in jeans and a black tank top. She blushed as he handed her the helmet he'd been wearing, then the keys with a wan grin.

La soldado, Marisol, rested her chin against the stock of a Remington Sendero bolt action rifle that was good enough to snipe a combatant or hunt *una cabra.* The barrel was heavy but made for accuracy, ensured by a Nightforce scope. She aimed between two targets standing at about two-hundred-fifty yards from where she was prone.

Marisol followed Agent Lopez since she had seen him earlier that day outside the US Attorney's office in San Juan. She had

213

commandeered someone's dirt bike to do so. With her finger resting outside the trigger guard, she watched and waited.

Lopez and the woman at the farm exchanged pleasantries and casual chuckles as the Remington's safety remained engaged. Marisol reminded herself that she had no interest in killing either of the two, even though with a few measured flinches of her fingers, she could make it happen.

The woman in the scope's sights offered something to the FBI agent, gesturing toward her lodge as if no one was pointing a rifle at her. It was really good for all involved when Lopez shook his head, declining. The woman only offered a hand to shake, which the FBI agent took.

Marisol gnawed the inside of her cheek when Lopez gave a polite, chaste peck of his lips to the woman's hand as if greeting a *quinceañera*. She switched off the safety and shook her head before reapplying it. Her FBI man only exchanged a few more words before he and the woman got in a weathered Ford pickup and headed away from *la hacienda*

La soldado stood and followed, easily keeping a casual distance. She'd had enough experience under the employ of drug dealers, wanna-be criminal entrepreneurs, and the like. Marisol could stalk or kill as needed. Her budding conscience clashed with old habits.

The pickup stopped near a bus station in Carolina. Lopez got out, nodding to the woman in the driver's seat with a smile before she drove off. *La soldado* used her Nightforce scope to follow him from a foliage-filled area under two hundred yards from the station. She wasn't sure what the best approach was, nor how to do so with the one-time prey who interested her, so she kept up surveillance as if on a hunt.

The focus of the Remington followed Lopez as he bought a

bus pass. As the sun was starting to pass beyond the western horizon, he waited to board bus T7 toward the Tren Urbano connecting metropolitan San Juan. A ruckus interrupted any peace.

Some punk came near, appearing to roughly pull a woman along with him. Lopez dropped everything he'd been holding and started toward the couple, ready to intervene. Rapid fire talk erupted between him and the thug, resulting in the belligerent boyfriend pulling a pistol.

Marisol did what came naturally. She pointed the Remington Sendero at the punk's package, exhaled and shot, knowing Lopez was in the line of fire if there was too much error. It was fortunate for the punk that her aim was slightly low. A .300 caliber round ripped through the thug's left calf before he fell to the ground.

Lopez took the thug's pistol and followed the line of fire to Marisol's location. Bus stop security was soon on top of *el gamberro* as the woman he'd been harassing looked on.

Not knowing what else to do, Marisol strapped the rifle to her back and got on the dirt bike, revving the engine to run off. Despite any training and instinct to the contrary, she failed to notice the sightseeing bus approaching her path until she had to make a split decision.

Marisol rolled off the bike before it slid to be crushed by the bus. Within minutes, the tourists had a story to tell, police had been called to respond, and she felt herself embracing gradual unconsciousness. Before emergency crews could respond, arms lifted her into some sort of vehicle.

"*Todo bien,*" Agent Lopez's voice said. *Me trajo un taxi.*" Don't worry. I called us a taxi.

215

* * *

Agent Roberto Lopez got off the couch early the next morning.

Yesterday, after a day at the office, he went to the horse farm to return Dr. Perez's dirt bike before taking a weekend. His commendation from Russo and his witness of events had put him on good footing with the brass in charge. A criminal complaint had put a target on his boss, Assistant Special Agent-in-Charge Rodriguo de Salinas, who was nowhere to be found.

Agent Lopez was welcome back to the FBI Monday morning. The Special Agent-in-Charge sought his leadership on an operation following local corruption. The Miami office was ready to coordinate, and Lopez was ready for a change of pace.

Any longing for his lioness soldier, guard, prey, lover and protector met a chance solution before he could make his way home. Upon having found her in the latter role outside the Carolina bus stop, he called a taxi for them before *la policía municipal* could get involved.

With fresh cleansing, care, and gauze, he had carried her to the bed to relax for rest the night. No need to include the authorities when dealing with scrupulous criminals.

As the sun presently showed itself along the eastern horizon, Agent Lopez wandered in his boxer briefs to his kitchenette to put instant Bustelo and water to a boil in a saucepan. He had a guest to accommodate. It was assumed she was still sleeping as he prepared food. A full breakfast would help the healing.

Lopez held a few *huevos* in front of the fridge, hoping to scramble them in a pan on his small gas stovetop until he felt the cold of metal along his spine. He considered that he may have made a poor choice until he heard a strong, female voice in his right ear, just where it met the neck. The metal was too rounded to be a knife.

"*Tranquilo y espera tu turno,*" said the voice. Relax. Wait your turn.

After permission, he reached a slow hand to turn off the burner. With no sudden movement, he turned around to see Marisol with a spatula in hand and a mouth mixed up in mischief. The T-shirt he'd lent her was already off.

A strong, slender set of hands soon wrapped around his waist to pull him toward her in a way that could make any guy happy. After a smack to his behind, the spatula and the eggs joined him and his guest on the vinyl floor to make a thud that wasn't nearly as impressive as the noises about to be made.

With his back on the floor, Marisol's sporty breasts and sinewy arms and shoulders tensed to keep Lopez pinned and excited. She writhed atop him until they were both out of breath. After the intense interlude, she lay his head on her chest in a way they hadn't done the evening in a stolen truck in a patch of wilderness off of the PR-52.

They lay for a while together, legs entwined, before she stood and ordered him to get on his feet.

After they donned underwear and stood together, she took more eggs from the fridge, handed them to him, and told him to get to work. Lopez did as told, instructing her on where she could get antiseptic and gauze to rewrap her wounds.

With her having done first aid and him having prepped *huevos, queso, and cafe,* they dined on a card table next to the kitchenette. Only wearing T-shirts and underwear, it was likely the most comfortable the two had felt in a while. A pleasant silence was only interrupted by the sounds of eating and children running around outside.

It was like the Hallmark imagery from a long-courting

couple, except that Lopez was an FBI agent and Marisol was job hunting with professional experience as a fixer, a soldier, *una soldado* for criminals. They'd come quite a ways from shooting at each other in the rain forest off the highway to San Juan.

Lopez broke the quiet, asking her what she was up to.

Marisol responded she was still figuring that out. A job from a respectable employer in need of kidnapping, assassination, and armed robbery skills would be nice. She chuckled before asking if the federal government was hiring.

Lopez smiled, speechless as she traced her toes up his calves and higher until it rested on his lap. He stayed quiet because he could not add anything attempting at wit. Marisol told him that on second thought, it might be best to handle her own affairs.

He didn't utter a word as he let the lady lead once again. She took his hand with a firm grasp, meandering toward the bedroom. *La soldado* was gentler than the feathery plumes inside the mattress, and he responded in kind. As the late morning sun's rays began to filter through the blinds, they lay naked together as the world outside buzzed with life.

"Me gustas." Marisol whispered into his ear. I'm pretty fond of you.

Roberto Lopez felt a lightening in his chest. He felt at peace, whatever that meant.

"Igualmente, " he muttered before drifting to unconsciousness. And I you.

* * *

Marisol stirred before the man lying beside her. She looked

at his reclining form, surveying muscles, tendons, and veins. At the time the FBI agent was most vulnerable, she realized ending his life was farther down her list than marriage and kids.

She recoiled at the thought of either prospect, which made her linger on the moment. Until recently, the focus of her life had been survival, making an employer happy, and the release she felt through ending or harming life. Admiring someone else, maybe caring for their welfare, was a new experience.

A range of new questions ran beneath Marisol's skin. This made her uncomfortable. The only response she had known before was to fight or flee, but this time there was a new feeling. She had to do a good deed before reverting to what was familiar. She got up and donned her underpants, her shorts, and one of his button-downs.

Marisol then put the dishes from breakfast in the sink. She mopped the floor before getting to the frying pan, the pot for the coffee, and the mugs and dishes. At the end of her tasks, she penned a note before stabbing it to the wall with a paring knife. With a smile and silent promise to stay in touch, she took her Remington rifle and left his home.

When Lopez awoke, his first sense was panic, which the cleaning and stabbed note didn't help. In time, he calmed himself and read the words.

"Igualmente, mi cariño. Siempre." it read. And I you, sweetie. Always.

The meaning wasn't entirely clear but welcomed adventures to come.

33

Rebuilding

Ron and Carey sat in the bed of the Ford pickup, laughing in each others' arms as they rode to the Equine Hacienda a little more than a week before the start of May. Margarita was driving in the cab as John rode shotgun. It was a Saturday, and they'd been spending the afternoon helping Margarita set up new digs by her niece.

Ron and John had outfitted an emptied horse shed on the *hacienda* grounds with a bathroom and makeshift kitchenette complete with a sink, a hot plate, and a mini refrigerator that ran from a small generator. It was at least as nice as Margarita's trailer and closer to family. They were all headed to the lodge to celebrate missions accomplished

The Ford stopped in the front, and Ron helped Carey out of the back, making sure she didn't bump her sling-laden arm. Margarita came around the back to kiss Ron's cheek and led John to help his mother.

The countryside was peaceful, with palms swaying in the breeze on either side of a dirt road. Dr. Maria Perez awaited *su tía* on her front stoop, smiling at a dear family member and her mainland friends.

Two of the gents Ron recognized from his encounter with Willy Ortiz also appeared, setting him on edge before Carey called them by name and chuckled. She seemed happy, and he remembered his wife's connections at the gun range with some *campesinos*.

Dr. Perez introduced the men to Ron as another figure joined the periphery. Willy Ortiz, the six-foot-tall solid tower of mahogany-skinned muscle first hugged Carey, wary of the hurt arm. He gave a shit-eating grin and offered a hand for Ron to shake, which was initially left hanging.

Ron faked a punch to Willy's gut, just slow enough for the gun nut to dodge. At a glance, there was an understanding that they had both hit below the belt in past dealings. The mahogany-skinned man apologized in a mixture of English and Spanish for lack of tact in battle.

Willy's brow furrowed before giving a sheepish look. He asked Dr. Perez to translate the message that he would be more gentle in the presence of *las mujeres y un niño*. Ron extended a hand, which Willy took. The two exchanged cordial if casually coerced grins before everyone peaceably entered Dr. Perez's lodge.

Ron pulled a seat for Carey and himself in the cozy dining room as the good doctor served them and her *tía* glasses with ice before Willy poured them a cool *cola con ron*. John got a limeade while the two *Boricuas* from the gun club got their own *bebidas*. Willy excused himself in Spanish, saying he had to tend to the spit-roast pig outside.

All gathered at a table help themselves to a mix of black beans, rice, and plantains cooked in cumin, crushed pepper, and butter. Willy was served a helping before coming inside with a platter of pulled-pork. He doled out the meat before serving himself. Before a bite was taken, Margarita led everyone in grace. Most of those present followed along. Willy and Ron were quiet out of respect.

Banter then zipped back and forth in Spanish and English as fast as rifle bullets in a battle zone. The seven adults at the table kept almost all of the jokes kid-friendly enough as John followed the conversation between bites. Carey only lightly kicked one of her friends under the table when he uttered a very vulgar word.

Margarita, Willy, and Dr. Perez stifled laughs as Ron and the other men exchanged oh-shit glances.

"*Lo siento,*" the man corrected himself. "*Estúpido.*"

John gave a toothy smile and everyone gave a chuckle.

When dinner was done, Ron offered his and John's services to help with dishes. Willy also offered help, exchanging smiles with Dr. Perez before the three men got busy in the kitchen. The women and Carey's gun club *campesino* friends went to the living room. The men were eager to show Carey their recently-purchased handguns.

Rapid Spanish echoed from the living room as the one with the loose tongue showed a Springfield XDM 9mm and the smarter one showed an ultralight titanium Taurus TCP .38. From the kitchen, Ron could hear his wife order them to field strip their firearms as safely and quickly as possible. When John, standing alongside him, began to whine, he told him to go watch mommy, expecting her to be in gun safety mode.

After a few seconds, Ron could hear the Taurus owner give a stunned yell after a smack to his hand, the skin-on-skin crack audible throughout the lodge. Carey went into a tempestuous tirade about the putz for forgetting to begin by checking for live rounds in the chamber. *Tanto, sangano,* and other terms of endearment could be heard.

John returned to the kitchen shortly thereafter, helping Dad and Willy clean dishes with a renewed vigor. Laughter between the women echoed from the other room as the Taurus owner apologized. Carey talked him through every step before the men in the kitchen finished their chores.

After everyone settled down, Ron and Carey announced they and John would soon be leaving Puerto Rico. After Russell Thurgood and seven other deaths from gunshot wounds a couple weeks ago at a Shelling-Polk-leased condo in San Juan, they felt it was best to move on. Gunfights in Fajardo and La Perla also made the decision easier. They were to go somewhere on the mainland for a fresh start.

Willy looked neutral, the two gun club guys seemed to understand after a translation, and Margarita and her niece nodded with approval. John vaguely knew what was going on, but trusted his parents more than anything. Everyone chatted about nothing in particular awhile before saying goodbyes.

Before the Rileys left out the front door. Carey called a taxi to take them to an Airbnb they'd rented in Carolina The gun club guys, Willy's helpers, fist bumped goodbyes and left in their own car. Margarita kissed everyone in the family on the cheek and wished them to feel at home in their new city as she felt in her new accommodations.

Dr. Perez shook all their hands and said goodbye before going to the lodge, first squeezing Willy on the abs. The mahogany-skinned man remained standing before the Rileys, a look of concern on his face.

"*Qué pasa,* Willy?" Carey asked.

EL campesino responded that he recalled another guy among

223

the others helping Thurgood, still alive from the explosions and gunfire in the Calle Norzagaray mid-rise. The casualty count from police weeks ago should have been nine, including the Shelling-Polk *pendejo*.

Fleeing police and the press had taken precedence, but Willy said he'd wished he'd had been more persistent. He added that after lifting Ron over his shoulder to descend stairs, and eventually dropping him, events were fuzzy. Willy had been too hurt at the time to follow up on a putz who ultimately knocked him out.

Ron, Carey and the farmer were quiet for a while, surprised at the man's look of unease. John interrupted, whining that he wanted to get going. Ron successfully signaled for quiet and spoke.

"We did the best we could, Willy," he continued with a look of assurance that cut across language. *"Nos dirigimos a casa y luego la parte continental. ¿A dónde vas?"* We are going home. Where are you headed for now?

Willy exchanged handshakes with Carey and John before smiling. He and Ron exchanged casual salutes before *el campesino* headed toward Dr. Perez's lodge.

When the taxi arrived, Ron held the door for his wife as she got in. He joined John in the back seat, counting stars on the way to Carolina. The night brought peace.

34

Panas

Carey awoke as the sun filtered through blinds the in the bedroom of their rental in the Isla Verde District of Carolina. With John in another bedroom and a balcony overlooking the northern coast, she was happy they'd found such a nice place for a small break, splurging a bit with insurance money from the incinerated place in Fajardo.

After escaping shootouts and kidnappings, dealing with insurance was easy, especially with a little federal help. She and her husband had made it out of another tight spot, and a sigh of relief and relaxation echoed a sense of calm from her chest to the rest of her body.

A light kiss below the ear woke Ron. His eyes blinked upon seeing his wife. The slope of her porcelain shoulders ran to a healthy bust under a soft, light comforter, framed by mild sunlight. She liked it when he grabbed her around the waist and spooned her gently, ever cautious of the cast holding her convalescing arm. He whispered about his love for her as his calloused hands rested on her smooth hips.

After a bit more than a snuggle in bed, Carey and Ron lay

together for a while. When they heard a rustle outside their door, they donned shorts, tank tops, and a sling for her before joining their son. Carey helped John get dressed as Ron headed to the kitchenette. Sunday breakfast was serious business.

John wandered to the table as potatoes steamed with chili powder and garlic in a saute pan. Ron gave him a smile before he sizzled *longaniza* sausage in a separate skillet and added eggs. When Carey entered, she used her unaffected arm to put on the Mr. Coffee and get her son some juice. The three of them breakfasted like any safe, happy family.

After cleaning the kitchenette and dishes, Ron and John they did their morning push ups and sit-ups, got washed, and dressed in shorts and tropical button-downs while Carey relaxed with her coffee. After she washed and donned khaki shorts and a light blue tank top, they all applied sunscreen before heading out for a walk on the beach.

It was a lazy morning.

After stopping around noon at the corner store to get both a fifth of Bacardi and Jim Beam, the Rileys caught a bus to see Officer Carlos Velez. Carey understood Ron had made a promise to his friend for helping them all and she didn't mind the company. Before leaving Puerto Rico within days, Ron was going to treat Carlos to drinks and dinner.

When the three arrived near Carlos's rental, they were surprised at what they saw. For another instance within the past few days, the unexpected was pleasant.

Carlos waved to them, smiling, before he kicked a soccer ball, passing it to one of two boys hanging in the alleyway outside. Neither Carey nor Ron had seen the man so happy before. One of the boys passed the ball to John. Ron remembered he had met the soccer companions weeks ago after the shootout in La Perla.

A slender woman, younger than Carey, soon exited the rental. She smiled bashfully, carrying sliced plantains marinading in a pan as Carlos tended to a grill.

After putting the starchy veggies on low-medium heat, Carlos soon offered everyone, Good O Kolas, spiking the adults' with the Bacardi.

La mujer helped the *niños* to sugary goodness, acting as a good guardian. All three boys gulped down the beverages before getting back to play, saying *gracias* after being prompted.

The adults sat in lawn chairs under an umbrella as the boys passed the ball in the sun. Carlos made formal introductions and handshakes were exchanged as the plantains cooked. The woman, Mia, smiled at Carey and Ron

"Mia was *la mujer* from La Perla we'd been looking for. Fortunately, *los uniformados* found her and she wasn't a casualty of the mess on Calle Norzagaray," Carlos told them. "Since her home was destroyed by gun-wielding *pendejos,* I've been working with a social worker to get her into public housing. She wanted to meet the nice *gringo* who played a part in helping her two nephews. I was in the mood for a cookout."

Ron's said in his basic Spanish that he was happy all the innocents made in through the mess safely; he was just doing his job. Carey took the woman's hands. Mia thanked Ron in rapid Spanish.

"*De nada, señora,*" Carey and Ron replied in unison.

After a short while of cordial chit chat, Carlos got the plantains. Carey and Ron found out that Mia used to work as a maid and had hung out with their state police friend for the past week to be a good influence. She had first visited Carlos's rental that day and found it charming.

Carey gave a knowing glance to her husband as Carlos served the plantains, offering drink refills. She snickered after Ron signaled that he would like a water and added he'd take care of things if his wife wanted to relax.

"I don't need permission," she responded, helping herself to a double.

Carey toasted Mia after *la mujer* had helped herself to another pouring. Carlos helped himself to a Jim Beam and Good O Kola before sitting next to Ron, handing his friend *una agua*. Carlos drank his bourbon and cola quickly before adding more whiskey to leftover ice cubes.

Carey watched the men get up after some time. Ron told her they were heading to the nearby grocery to pick up some steaks. Her hubby and their friend needed some space, and all the adults could feel it. The fellas seemed to grow more chatty as they headed down the block.

She got up from her chair to grab two Medalla Lights from a cooler as Mia got more cola for her nephews and John. The two sat back down with the beers, toasting to their health as the boys spoke rapidly among themselves. John appeared to be fitting in nicely.

* * *

Just east of the Parque Barbosa, where greenery and a slight wind allowed a brief oasis from the heat, Ron felt himself relax. Carlos seemed to calm upon the small sojourn away from what he rather poetically called the unfamiliar, fitted noose of domestic bliss. *El uniformado* also seemed to walk a little straighter after giving the booze a rest.

"*Qué tal, mano?*" Ron asked. "What's up? You looked pretty

happy with a few *niños* hanging in your yard and that nice *mujer*."

"I'm used to keeping a cool head at work," Carlos said. "I miss letting it snap when off the clock. There's complications now. This *chica* has her own baggage, including the two *chicos* she looks after. Life was simpler when I just could get shitfaced and enjoy some *mujerzuelas*."

Ron and his friend stopped before getting to the end of the park. Carlos was only a few years younger, but Ron saw a less mature self coupled with a 1980s Jimmy Smits look. The Army veteran, former strip club bouncer, and part-time tough guy-for-hire oddly now seemed the more stable of the two, despite *el uniformado's* steady job and expected promotion to sergeant.

"Maybe you want more than a *mujerzuela*. You never went to bed with any call girls, despite engaging some as informants," Ron said. "I don't believe this *macho* talk I'm hearing from you: *tú hablas paja*. It's all bullshit."

Carlos appeared more serious. He turned on his heel and returned the same stink eye from in El Rococo when Ron had served his men booze. The *gringo* stood firm, using a good four inches height.

"You want me to patronize you or respect you, *cabrón?*" Ron said. "Come on, let's get some steaks."

They both broke out in a chuckle as Carlos faked a smack to his friend's stomach.

The two soon traded any freedom of environment for the claustrophobic confines of a supermarket off Calle McLeary, squeezed in a number of blocks from the beach. Calm seemed to come over Carlos while Ron grew uneasy.

Inside the Plaza Loiza, the friends passed aisles stocked with cans of Goya canned vegetables, produce people wouldn't find in Middle America, Bustelo, and Good O Kola before arriving mercifully at *la carnicera*. For Ron, the display was similar to what he remembered from the Humboldt Park Cermak when he lived in Chicago.

In an assured baritone, Carlos picked out some juicy porterhouse steaks, quipping to the butcher that the *gringo* was paying. The man behind the counter wiped blood off the meat and prepped it in peppercorn and garlic before weighing and wrapping it. Ron paid and they headed back to the cookout.

Walking back across the park, Ron asked Carlos to listen and carry the steaks as he talked about the way Carey made him better. He cared about the future and found a new feeling of home. He planned to leave in a few days to help protect that family, even promising willing cooperation with a friend in law enforcement.

"You think you have some wisdom to deliver, *viejo*," Carlos deadpanned.

"I don't have all the answers," Ron replied, looking at his friend, "but I've seen a lot and I know what works."

Carlos should at least learn to live life, use his ethic outside of work, and sleep with someone who challenges him to be better, he said. *Los niños y la mujer* seemed to make Sergeant Velez laugh and look more human.

"Do right by those who depend on you," Ron said, realizing he was more giving himself a talk than his *amigo*.

"Preach, my brother," Carlos said with a chuckle. "I think I heard that on one of those God channels. You might make the big bucks for *su mujer y su hijo* telling other *gringos* how to live life right."

"Okay, *pendejo*. *Me bajaré de mi tribuna.* I'll get off my soapbox. I'm still figuring stuff out myself, but I've been there."

"I hear you, *mano*," Carlos said. "Let's just try to have a good time in my hood before you leave the island like a snitch fleeing stitches."

Ron laughed at the attempted line, likely learned from pirated movies.

Banter turned to football, soccer, and drinking stories for the rest of the walk. They laughed instead of sulking on a sunny Sunday.

As late afternoon approached back at Carlos's rental, *el uniformado* grilled the steaks to perfection and Ron sipped a Beam and water on ice. Pink flushed Carey's cheeks as she practiced her Spanish with Mia. John gave his stepdad a fist bump before he joined the other boys to watch meat grill on fire.

*Los niño*s all seemed entranced, even more so when Carlos delivered a porterhouse steak to each of Mia's nephews on paper plates before serving one to John. The adults chuckled before joining the boys around a small table. Ron helped John cut his to bits before helping his wife. They all ate, too busy to talk. The men cleaned afterward.

As the sun started its descent toward the horizon, Carlos surprised all the boys with sparklers. He stayed with them as they ran around. Ron monitored John, staying close behind.

"*Necesitamos música*," Mia said to Carey before she got a portable radio from the home. She set it to an oldies and standards station, with bolero and salsa numbers.

Carey watched, amused and engaged, as *la mujer* from La Perla swayed gracefully in time with the music in her chair. Entranced with the music, they both stood and danced.

When the boys returned, both ladies were swaying along

with the cheeky trumpet in "Dos Gardenias." Mia's nephews and John returned to passing a ball nearby as Ron and Carlos's attention focused on *las mujeres hermosas*.

As the sky became a hue between tangerine and peach, Ron watched the sway of Carey's hips to the melody before joining her. He lifted the hand of her uninjured arm before placing his other hand on the small of her back. His eyes locked on the hazel hue opposite him. Her button nose wrinkled with a touch of mischief.

Carlos looked the wallflower as Mia glanced at him and smiled. When the delicious, smooth guitar and bass intro of "Bésame Mucho" led to the sultry voice of Consuelito Velázquez, he asked Mia to dance.

Their host displayed the manners of a gentleman from 1940, when the song was written. Mia took his right hand and put it above her hip, leading with his other hand in hers, her left on his shoulder.

The couples' pace picked up with Ismael Rivera's "El Nazareno," with Ron barely keeping up with Carey's steps. She gave a belly laugh before allowing him to stop and lean in for a deep kiss on the lips.

Mia and Carlos kept up with the melody without a problem. Ron helped Carey to a chair before going to retrieve their son. It was time to call it a night.

He returned with the boys as Mia and Carlos were wrapping up a lively salsa from Willie Rosario. All three boys danced crazily around the couple after initial groaning. When the song came to an end, Mia gave her nephews jesting slaps on the behinds before tousling John's hair. Carlos then turned down the music, seeing cues from his guests.

Mia kissed Ron and Carey on the cheeks before bumping

fists with John and taking her nephews by the shoulders. She gave a look to Carlos and then to the rental as if trying to gauge the policeman's thoughts

"*Quédate la noche aquí*," Carlos said. *"El sofá estará bien para mí."* Stay the night. The couch is fine for me.

Mia rolled her eyes, blew kisses to the Rileys, gave a flirty smirk to *el uniformado*, and took her nephews inside. Those still saying goodbye embraced the calm for several minutes, only charmed with the soft bolero music lingering in the background.

"Well, *cabrón*, it looks like you'll have your hands full," Ron said. " You'll be fine, though."

"*Gracias, mano.*" Carlos responded. He then offered Ron and Carey handshakes, which Ron took before Carey gave a hug. John exchanged fist bumps. After *el uniformado* returned to his rental for relaxation, recreation, or a little bit of both, the Rileys grabbed a bus back toward Isla Verde.

Once back at their Airbnb, Ron and Carey put John to bed before returning to their room. They stripped, washed, and put on clean T-shirts before getting the best rest they'd had in a while. The rumble of the shore nearby lulled them to sleep.

35

Nice and Safe

Over an expanse of mangroves and sawgrass protecting crawfish, crabs, and mackerel in the Everglades from egrets, kingfishers, and osprey, twin propellers hummed on a Cessna 421c as it lowered itself to the earth.

Special Supervisory Agent Matt Russo stood in a hangar at Homestead General Airport, a hand shielding his eyes from late afternoon sunlight. The US Marshal Service deemed the airfield a suitable place to reconnect briefly with Russo's asset. They'd last seen each other almost a month earlier.

Russo predicted Ron Riley's glare and flinch when a US Marshall offered a hand out of the Cessna, which made the agent chuckle just the same. Ron emerged with two suitcases in each hand before putting one on the ground. Carey took an arm from her husband to disembark next, still careful about her cast. John jumped onto the tarmac, seeming not to feel the weight his backpack.

A US Marshall, dressed in a navy blue suit, escorted the Rileys toward Russo. Matt, in an FBI blazer that was too formal for the heat, shook hands with the government functionary when they were all together.

It was understood the FBI agent's presence was off the books, unofficial, and unsanctioned. Russo had turned off all GPS on his phone and Ford Taurus for his just under an hour southeast drive from the Miami field office.

"So, when do we get to see Disney's Magic Kingdom?" Ron asked. "And Hooters? John and I need to get some wings and see if we can still get Carey's employee discount."

"Forget this *pendejo*," Carey said before Russo could manage a comeback. "I only stay with him for the security and the money. How are you doing, Matt?"

Russo clapped Ron on the shoulder and got a cordial kiss on the cheek from Carey before tousling John's hair.

"Good to see you're in charge, Carey," he said. "As Clara and Zoe expect me home for dinner, and my higher-ups don't know about this meeting, I'll have to keep it short."

Russo explained a US Marshal would take them their new home, the location of which he didn't know. He handed Ron a locked briefcase, then handed Carey a lockbox, and gave a key to John before continuing.

The Rileys could find any needed information in their packages and instructions on how to keep in touch. Russo had to stay blind to some aspects of his friends, to ensure their safety because of friction between various competing federal government agencies.

"You remind me of the Army enlistment officer I met after college," Ron said after a pause. "Friendly, but not anyone I'd want to drink with."

"I gave up the sauce, anyway," Russo replied "I've since been less of an asshole. Maybe you could try doing the same, Ron?"

The two men exchanged smirks before a solid handshake.

Russo wished them well and told Ron to check in when he could through an unofficial line. John and Carey grinned before he watched a different US Marshal pull up in a black Ford Expedition. The Rileys were escorted inside, luggage put in the back.

Russo then got in his Ford Taurus and headed home. The drive went slowly, plodding along with NPR news updates. Of note on the radio, pharmaceutical company Shelling-Polk had just merged its Puerto Rico assets into Merck. The new spokesman, Jimmy Ocasio, announced in heavily-accented English that Merck's acquisition proposed a healthy future for stable growth and local jobs.

The spokesman's name rang familiar from when Russo was liaising with San Juan FBI, and he made a mental note to check on it next time he was at the Miami office.

For now, he had to change the radio station to classic rock to get the Led out. A few chews of Nicorette helped him relax. When he pulled near Coconut Grove, he was famished.

The sight of his wife and daughter welcomed him home.

* * *

The US Marshal, whose name was George, drove the Ford Expedition north on the Ronald Reagan Turnpike past Miami. Green fields, forests, and swamps whizzed by on either side as Ron and Carey opened their packages.

Ron groaned when he found the iPhone among a ring of keys. He handed Carey the so-called phone before taking a note from a sealed envelope.

The note, signed by their friend Russo, gave some info on the new life the US Marshal Service had arranged for the Rileys, including checking account numbers with some capital to get started.

Per the note, the keys were for a Toyota Prius, a new rental home, and a safe inside the master bedroom. Ron was to report to Crossroads Investigations the following Monday and would be able to communicate with Russo via an anonymous Skype handle preloaded in an app on the iPhone. Info on a job for Carey and education for John was forthcoming.

The Rileys were quiet throughout most of the hour drive, with Carey trying to perk the boys up when the Explorer pulled to an off-ramp. Ron gave his wife and son a wan grin as a sign for Sunrise, Florida came into view. On streets somewhat like that of Naperville, a sense of familiarity washed over Ron's face as the Expedition rolled by rows of identical, ranch-style houses.

The US Marshal, George, pulled alongside one of the driveways, bringing the SUV to a stop. He unloaded suitcases, politely shaking the Rileys' hands before leaving.

The family walked across the driveway to the new digs after Ron looked left and Carey looked right toward the stream of sameness that struck them as more soul-sucking than safe. No other families were outside.

"A little over a year ago we escaped the suburbs," Ron said, before turning the key in the front lock. "I'm not sure it's so great to be back."

"The plus side is no one is trying to kidnap or kill us, at least for now," Carey deadpanned as they stood outside. "Also, the weather is pleasant enough."

Ron groaned before his wife gave him a small smack to the shoulder with her untethered forearm.

John suddenly pulled at his mom's shorts and called out. The look on his face was serious as he asked in Spanish to see Mia's cousins. The innocence drew in the focus of his parents.

Carey crouched to his level, explaining in English that they'd have to see what the future brought. She said he, she, and Dad had to figure things out now and see about visiting after some time.

"What can we do now?" she asked him.

"I want to play football," John said after a pause for thought.

Ron held up a finger before heading inside. His wife and son waited outside as he paid no attention to anything else except finding a soccer ball. He found an inflated red ball most kids used for kickball. It would have to do.

After opening the garage door and side-stepping the Prius, Ron emerged with the kickball.

"Who's ready for a game?" Ron asked.

"Yeah!" John said with a look of glee.

The three Rileys set up goals with Mom and Dad's shoes on the front lawn, which allowed them a small playing field thirty feet long. Carey stayed on the sidelines and ran as a referee, her arm still in a cast.

Though Ron was in shape, John was a phenom in the making, dribbling and darting through to the goal. After a good forty-five minutes sprinting back and forth, they declared John the winner, 4-2.

After a quick stretch, the three collected the ball and Mom and Dad's shoes before heading inside. Carey and John found showers to wash up as Ron removed his T-shirt and scavenged the pantry in hopes WITSEC staff had stocked basic provisions.

He found a few cans of SpaghettiOs and a bag of salad in the fridge. A Brita pitcher held water. No cold beer awaited. It would have to do.

Carey emerged in a bathrobe a little while later. John emerged from the other bathroom shortly after, wearing Bob the Builder pajamas. They tended to dinner as Ron retreated to what Carey chose as their bathroom to wash up.

After cool water rinsed off lather, Ron could hear Carey yelling for help in the other room. He exited at once, wrapping a towel around his waist.

John was safe but looked concerned as Carey held their new iPhone with her good hand, her thumb scrolling across the screen. Ron rushed to shut off the stove top, saving dinner and preventing immediate problems. He asked his wife what was the matter.

About the Author

Ben Broeren is a native of Wisconsin and has a couple of degrees from the University of Wisconsin-Madison. He has worked as a freelance writer for newspapers and alternative weeklies in Chicago and Madison, Wisconsin. His journalism has been published in *Isthmus, The Capital Times*, and *New City*.

In addition to journalism and academia, he has experience as a dishwasher, a kitchen assistant, a cook, a warehouse tractor driver, a mail clerk, a hotel clerk, a personal service assistant for disabled adults, a bookseller, a tutor, a volunteer for a presidential campaign, a volunteer legal clerk for a civil rights firm, and a volunteer for WORT community radio. He currently works at a Chicago Public Library branch as a technology and jobs assistant for patrons.

He lives with his wife, his son, and his dog in the Bridgeport neighborhood of Chicago. When not writing, editing, and working, he likes to cook various types of cuisine, read, ride his recumbent trike, and keep up with what's going on through the news and talking with neighbors.

You can connect with me on:

🌐 https://www.bendbroeren.com

🄵 https://www.facebook.com/BDBroeren

Also by Ben Broeren

Ben Broeren's books are available at Chicago Public Library and Neenah Public Library in his Wisconsin hometown. They can be ordered at most bookstores.

Ben writes to explore history, his mental state, and multiple views of the world we find ourselves in. He hopes his readers not only find and an entertaining escape, but discover humor and passions that drive all our stories.

A Racket in the Burbs (Carey and Ron #1)

Ron McCallister's job is to be a hard-ass, to keep unwelcome degenerates out of Starlet's Alley. The strip club is one of the only locally owned business in Chicago's suburb of Woolrich. The pay beats working anywhere else nearby, and Ron can keep tabs on the city's scum, both well-connected and otherwise.

Ron's life changes when a stripper who piques his interest, Carey Sullivan, saves his life from sleazy mob subordinates. The brush with death pits both of them against municipal politicians, local police, and the mobsters who own them.

Carey and Ron rely on their wits, a growing cadre of like-minded friends, and a little outside help to strike back at local thugs and attempt to take back their lives. During their struggle, a desire ignites between them that burns brighter than a freshly-lit Molotov cocktail.

North Side Hellion

Aiden McCarthy enjoys thieving and scheming much more than abiding by the morals of his Catholic, Irish American, working-class parents. He has always been a pisser, but working for the North Side Gang feeds his youthful desire for action, rebellion, and romance.

When Aiden's father is injured in crossfire between Italian gangsters, he must balance adventure with duty to family. With his interest in the daughter of one of the Italians and a sense of justice in the midst of gangland competition, he must find his way through undercurrents of lust, social upheaval, and rebellion against Prohibition.

Aiden McCarthy's story intertwines with Irish-American gang leader Dean O'Banion, a young Alphonse Capone, John Torrio, and other historical figures in this Jazz Age tapestry to satisfy adventure-seekers, romantics, and history-lovers alike.

www.ingramcontent.com/pod-product-compliance
Lightning Source LLC
Chambersburg PA
CBHW021008120726
47905CB00009B/2904